THE BATTLE FOR OZ

JEYNA GRACE

THE BATTLE FOR
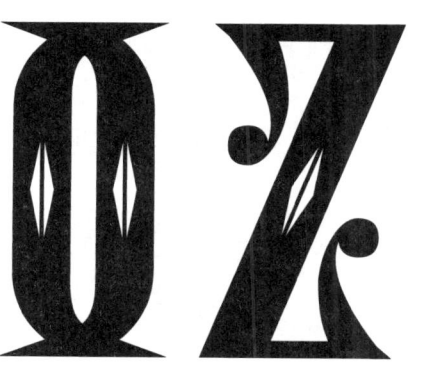

INKSHARES

This is a work of fiction. Names, characters, organizations, places, events, and incidents are either products of the author's imagination or are used fictitiously.

Copyright © 2015 Jeyna Grace

All rights reserved.

No part of this book may be reproduced, or stored in a retrieval system, or transmitted in any form or by any means, electronic, mechanical, photocopying, recording, or otherwise, without express written permission of the publisher.

Published by Inkshares Inc., San Francisco, California
www.inkshares.com

Edited and designed by Girl Friday Productions
www.girlfridayproductions.com
Cover design by David Drummond

Cover images © wowomnom/Shutterstock, © Fona/Shutterstock, © ILeysen/Shutterstock

ISBN: 9781941758311
Library of Congress Control Number: 2015938854

First edition

Printed in the United States of America

Dedicated to the heroes inside all of us.

1
EXITIUM

CHAPTER 1

The court erupted in angry shouts of agreement. The spectators urged that she be immediately banished to the wastelands—and there was nothing she could say or do to convince them otherwise. Even her husband did not speak in her defense. She was done for.

Before the sun set, she was escorted out of the kingdom. A crowd gathered in the streets to bid her a jeering farewell. She knew they would celebrate when she was gone. It was infuriating, but she was no longer the one who could order their banishment—this time it was she who'd been banished.

As she left the now-happy kingdom behind, most of her feathered guards followed her. Although she told them they could stay and celebrate, they understood the implied threat. Oh, how she enjoyed their nervous and silent company.

When they reached the black, flat, foul-smelling wastelands, her guards found her a large rabbit hole that led to a giant burrow. She was ready to strike them for considering such an unfit shelter for a woman of her status, but held back her hand when she found a motherless litter of muttbits curled up together in the burrow.

Muttbits were like dogs but had pointed, rabbit-like ears, long whiskers, and two sharp front teeth. Due to their wild, aggressive behavior, they'd been banished from the kingdom. She'd always thought they were revolting, but now that she was able to identify with them, she thought they might make good pets. She also had an idea—a crazy idea she was not going to let go of.

The muttbits were strangely welcoming toward her when she invaded their home, probably because she fed them raw meat. While she bonded with her newfound friends, her guards made the reeking place livable. They placed torches around the cave-like burrow and stacked a pile of pillows in a corner for her sleepy head. They even sprayed some perfume in the air in the hopes of ridding the space of its nose-scrunching smell.

The burrow, with a rather high ceiling and plenty of space, was a suitable enough home in the wastelands, but she knew she could not stay. How could a royal live in such a godforsaken place? She might have been—as the court had called her earlier that day—insane, but she wasn't stupid. This burrow was merely a temporary home until she found a new one—a new palace, to be precise.

She held back the mad urge to reclaim her throne and took her time raising and breeding her muttbits. Two weeks later, they had doubled in number. Half the pups were as big as full-grown bears. Her guards were terrified of them because they snapped violently anytime the guards approached. But when it came to her, the muttbits were angels. She was convinced they saw her as their mother, and she soon started calling them her babies.

Once she had raised an army of muttbits, she knew the time had come. She could now reclaim the throne and be queen again. With her muttbits fighting for her, she would regain her power. But she wasn't going to fight for the same throne. Instead, she had found another land filled with powerful magic that she coveted: Oz.

She had first learned about Oz in a book at the royal library. It was a place of magical creatures, picturesque mountains, lush forests, and a city made of a stone that looked like green glass called *emerald*. Although green wasn't her favorite color, jewels were definitely her favorite accessories.

On top of that, there was powerful magic in Oz, magic that she could use to seek revenge on those who had banished her. *Oh, wouldn't that be glorious?* she thought with a smile plastered on her fair face.

The fantasies floating around in her head excited her, and when she could not contain herself any longer, she ordered her guards to bring her small velvet pouch. Had anyone known what was in that pouch, she would have been banished much earlier.

Weeks before her trial she'd snuck into the royal archives, where artifacts from different realms were displayed in glass cases. There she'd stolen the tail of a winged monkey that was supposedly from Oz. She'd burnt it and mixed it with black fairy dust, then poured the dust into the pouch. According to her findings in various magic books, the powdery substance should take her to Oz.

Rounding up her guards and muttbits, she placed the small pouch in the center of the burrow. The guards waited for a special spell of some sort, but instead she ordered, "Burn it!"

The guards who were unfortunate enough to be standing near the torches pulled them from their sconces and walked up to the pouch. As they lowered the flames, the pouch immediately caught on fire, but nothing else happened. After a few minutes, she was sure the magic had failed, and her chest began to bubble in anger. When her disappointment was about to burst into fury, a deafening pop startled her angry heart.

The velvet pouch exploded into a large black cloud that began to swirl. The air in the burrow was still, and all eyes were glued in fascination to the dust devil. The guards standing in the center unfortunately had only a brief moment of awe before they were pulled into the rapidly growing tornado. The guards screamed, the muttbits growled, and hysterical laughter escaped her lips. The magic was working, and she couldn't be happier.

As the tornado burst through the burrow's ceiling, it swept everyone off their feet. A few seconds later the tornado was gone, and the wastelands returned to their usual silence. The only difference was a big hole in the ground that no one would ever likely discover.

CHAPTER 2

The tornado stopped swirling, and they landed on soft green grass in an open field. Almost immediately after touching the ground, she jumped to her feet and examined her surroundings. Everything was green except for a gravel road that cut through an open field, which dropped off over the hillside.

"Everyone, on your feet!" she ordered.

As her guards scrambled up, one of them almost had his arm bitten off when he stepped on a muttbit's tail. Not even waiting for the commotion to die down, she started along the road.

The sun was high in the bright-blue sky, and the birds were chirping a harmonious melody. She had no complaints about the warm sun, as it lifted her mood and convinced her of a sure win. As she descended the slope in the road, she smiled. She saw a bright-green city not too far away, sparkling in the sunshine. Its majestic glory sent shivers down her spine. Emerald City would soon be hers, and she couldn't be more excited.

As they headed toward the city, one of her guards boldly asked, "What is the plan, Your Highness?"

"You'll see," she replied with a mischievous grin.

When they finally reached the tall glass gate to Emerald City, the uniformed soldiers standing guard approached her. They looked friendly but nonetheless slightly suspicious. She didn't snap at them the way she usually did back home.

Smiling, she said, "I'm a queen from a neighboring realm, and I'm here to make peace with Oz."

The soldiers nodded, eyeing the muttbits closely. One soldier disappeared behind a small door, and another said, "We are pleased to have you, Your Highness. We will inform Queen Ozma of your visit."

When the soldier made no move to let her in, she asked in a falsely sweet tone, "May I not enter your great city?"

"Oh, of course you may. We are just not too sure of your . . ." He trailed off, uncertain what to call them.

"They are harmless—they just have trust issues," she replied.

The soldier nodded but still refused to let her in. She had no choice but to wait. Finally, after a long, uncomfortable silence, the tall glass gate opened, releasing the sound of a lively crowd. Queen Ozma appeared, along with an older woman and a group of soldiers. If it weren't for the shiny crown on the girl's head, she would have thought the older woman was the queen.

"Your Highness," Queen Ozma greeted her.

"Your Highness," she replied with a slight nod.

"I hear you have come a long way to make peace with Oz. I am very honored to make your acquaintance," Queen Ozma said. The young queen, who wasn't even a teenager yet, wore a simple green-and-gold dress that matched her city almost perfectly.

"The honor is all mine. All I want is the best for both our realms," she answered.

Although the young queen was convinced by her act, the older woman wasn't. She wore a white dress—clearly not a symbol of youth—and a diamond necklace that glowed light green.

"This is Glinda, my most trusted advisor and a powerful witch," Queen Ozma said when she saw her looking at the older woman.

She nodded at the introduction and patiently waited to be invited in. It did not take long—Queen Ozma soon made an irresistible offer.

"Why don't you join me for tea, and we can discuss our treaty," Queen Ozma said. "I'm sure you will love our teatime snacks."

"I would love to," she replied and followed the queen.

They cut through a large market on their way to the palace. When the people saw their queen, they immediately stepped aside and kneeled, shouting praise and well-wishes. She could get used to such treatment.

Upon reaching the golden palace gates, Glinda whispered to Queen Ozma. If only she knew their visitor had such a powerful sense of hearing, she would not have bothered whispering.

"Your Highness, those creatures don't look too friendly. Why don't they wait in their own room while you talk to their queen?"

"Surely you don't expect me to enjoy my visit unprotected?" she interjected. She had not liked Glinda from the moment she saw her.

"Of course not," Queen Ozma quickly replied.

"I understand your worries," she said, "but at least let me take one of my pets with me. The rest can wait."

"Oh, sure. Please do," Queen Ozma said.

Glinda again whispered her objections. While the two bickered softly, she turned to her biggest muttbit and gently stroked its head. She cleared her throat to interrupt the small argument between the two women and snapped her fingers. Her chosen muttbit stepped closer to her.

"What an adorable little creature," Queen Ozma said, attempting praise.

"He sure is," she replied.

Glinda attempted to protest again but stopped when Queen Ozma led them into the royal garden. The old witch found her threatening. That itself was the first sign of victory. She hid a little smile.

The royal garden was filled with colorful flowers and shady trees. Dragonflies zoomed across the glistening water of a small pond. A table in the middle of the garden was covered with plates of sweets, neatly arranged around a glass teapot in the center.

"Please sit," Queen Ozma said as she took her seat.

She joined her at the table, keeping her muttbit close. It sat between them, and the uneasiness of the situation showed on Glinda's face, who stood a few feet away. Queen Ozma did not seem to have the slightest clue how badly things could go—the second sign of victory.

"I'm so sorry, but I didn't catch your name," Queen Ozma said as a servant filled their teacups.

"My people call me Queen," she said, cautious to not reveal her true identity.

"Oh, that's interesting. So, Queen, which realm are you from?"

"I am so glad you asked," she paused, taking her time before answering. "I'm from Oz."

"Oz? Is there another realm called Oz?" Queen Ozma asked, turning toward Glinda.

"Oh no, there's only one. And I intend to be its new queen."

CHAPTER 3

The next few moments happened in a flash.

Everything happened so fast that the guard standing nearby didn't even have a second to react. Her muttbit leapt onto Queen Ozma and pinned her down, and Glinda instinctively pulled out her wand and pointed it at the muttbit.

But a spell didn't shoot toward the bear-sized creature. Everything came to a standstill after the split second of chaos. Glinda hesitated. The muttbit's mouth hovered, open, over Queen Ozma's neck. All the creature needed to do was shut its heavy jaws, and the young queen would be dead.

Glinda's hesitation was the third sign of victory. It was now right outside her door.

"Oh my, I'm so sorry. My muttbit has trust issues," she said.

"What do you want?" Glinda demanded calmly.

Queen Ozma was sobbing, her face turned away from the ugly creature.

"Didn't I tell you already? I want to be the new queen of Oz."

"Do you think you can just take the throne?" Glinda asked.

"Of course I can, unless you want to feed your queen to my pet," she said with a smile.

Glinda looked aghast but defeated. The self-proclaimed new queen stood up and walked over to her. She took the wand from her hand and snapped it in two. She then reached for her necklace, but Glinda pushed her hand away.

"You can't take this," Glinda said.

She didn't reply. Instead, she turned to her muttbit and asked, "Are you hungry, baby?"

Her muttbit gave a low growl, its saliva dripping onto the young queen's fragile neck.

It was a good enough threat. Glinda pulled the necklace off and handed it to her.

"Thank you," she said cheerfully as she removed the diamond. "Now, for my first decree! I shall be known as the New Queen of Oz. Those who fail to obey me will die."

"Please let Queen Ozma go," Glinda said.

"Don't interrupt me!" the New Queen shouted.

She clutched the diamond in her palm and pointed her finger at Glinda. Just as the New Queen expected, a spell shot from her finger and struck Glinda on the throat. Within a second, a vine with sharp thorns appeared and twisted around her neck, choking her.

The young queen screamed for help, but no one came to the rescue. The soldiers were afraid for Queen Ozma's and Glinda's safety but scared of facing the same fate.

"Don't kill her!" Queen Ozma screamed, ignoring the angry growls of the muttbit.

"I won't," the New Queen said, undoing the spell. When Glinda could finally gasp for air, she passed out.

The New Queen couldn't believe how easy it had been. She now had the most powerful magic in her hand and could do with it what she chose. As the diamond glowed in her palm, she felt the surge of power through her body. She now knew how weak Glinda had been, especially since she'd needed a wand to channel her magic. But, of course, she was different. She was still fresh, both young and powerful, and very ready to rule.

"Summon the rest, baby," she commanded her muttbit.

With Queen Ozma still pinned beneath it, the muttbit raised its head and gave a loud, long howl. Queen Ozma's guards were forced to give way to the intruders as they responded to their queen's call. When the New Queen's guards arrived, she ordered them to take Glinda to the dungeons. Then she sweetly asked Queen Ozma to show her the queen's chamber.

Queen Ozma didn't have much choice. Walking behind her, the New Queen rested her heavy hands, full of magic, on the young queen's shoulders. Three large, growling muttbits tailed them.

As the New Queen strutted down the hallway, no one tried to stop her. The soldiers could only watch as she took over the royal palace. It didn't take them long to realize that they'd be torn in two if they attempted to fight back—even without the New Queen's magic. She was no doubt a genius to have bred a little army of muttbits.

When they finally reached the queen's chamber, the New Queen was pleased to find the huge room so beautifully decorated.

"It looks like I won't need to redecorate," she said.

There was a wide bed covered in silk sheets, a fireplace, and a skillfully carved dressing table. In the corner stood a tall mirror framed in green glass. The intricate carvings in the frame looked beautiful in the sunlight shining in through an open window.

"Ozma," the New Queen said, "I've found your new home."

The young queen looked at her, confused. "What are you talking about?"

"Don't you like this mirror? I think it's wonderful," she said as she walked toward it.

"My father had it made for my mother."

"So you like it, of course."

"Yes," Queen Ozma replied reluctantly. The New Queen could tell she was trying to come up with an escape plan, but unfortunately for her, she wasn't escaping anytime soon.

"Good. Because that's where you're going!" the New Queen announced.

Queen Ozma didn't understand what she meant until the New Queen touched the mirror with the diamond. As it made contact, the mirror turned into a silvery liquid. The New Queen pushed her finger through the mirror just to test it, then smiled broadly.

"What are you going to do?" Queen Ozma began to panic.

"Don't worry, it won't hurt a bit."

The New Queen pointed at Queen Ozma's chest and used her magic to pull her toward the mirror. The young queen tried to free herself, but she was paralyzed, her legs frozen. No matter how hard she struggled, the force was too strong.

When Queen Ozma was an inch away from the silvery liquid, the New Queen reached for her crown. She placed it on her own head, then gave the young queen a slight push. Queen Ozma disappeared into the liquid.

A moment later, the mirror returned to its original form, with Queen Ozma inside. She was trapped behind the reflection of her own bedchamber and couldn't get out. She screamed and pounded her fists against the glass, but no one could hear her.

The New Queen watched for a few minutes, laughing. When she finally grew tired, she clapped her hands together and said, "It's time to make Oz mine. But first, we must plan a celebration!"

CHAPTER 4

Preparations took a long, torturous week. The citizens of Oz, forced to work for the New Queen, turned the green city red. From the floors to the windows, everything had to change. Only the glass city wall remained the same color—not even magic could change it.

It was still green around Emerald City, but stepping through the city gate was like walking into a different realm. The cheerful lampposts were replaced with red lanterns, and new crimson royal banners hung at every corner. The soldiers no longer wore green and gold but red and gold. The city, filled with red yet surrounded by green walls, looked like Christmas came early—but it felt much less joyful.

In the center of the giant courtyard that separated the citizens' homes from the royal palace, the New Queen replaced the giant fountain of dancing lights with a solid-gold statue of herself. On the day of the celebration, hundreds of tables draped in red cloth were placed around the statue. A long table with a row of empty chairs faced an uncomfortable-looking jeweled armchair.

When night finally fell in Oz, the citizens began to fill the courtyard. None of them wanted to be there, but it was either death or dinner, and everyone preferred the latter. Leaders of the countries that neighbored Oz were also invited and seated by the

New Queen. Unlike a normal celebration, this one lacked cheer or excitement. Once everyone found their seats, silence fell as though it were a funeral.

After a few minutes of pin-drop silence, the New Queen appeared wearing an elegant red dress. Nobody said a thing as she descended the long flight of stairs and passed through the palace gates to the courtyard. She smiled as she waved, flaunting the magical diamond that she now wore as a ring on her index finger.

The New Queen had expected her people to cheer, so the quiet was making her blood pressure rise. She forced herself to stay calm as she sat down in the jeweled armchair. Suppressing her burning desire to curse everyone present, she loudly clapped her hands twice.

The waiters in red began serving the first dish of the night, rose duck with spicy applesauce. Once she and the honored guests were served, she turned to them and asked, "How do you like Oz's new look?"

"Wonderful!" said a thin man in a purple suit with fake excitement.

"Is purple your favorite color?" the New Queen asked without hiding her disgust.

"It's—it's the color of my people, Your Highness. We Gillikins—"

"I don't care about you Gillikins," the New Queen interrupted. She eyed him closely as she waited for an apology, but he was tongue-tied with terror.

Just when she was about to chastise him further about his choice of color, a loud crash came from the other end of the table, where a man with wheels for hands sat.

"Apologies, Your Highness," he said, bowing his head.

"You're a Wheeler, aren't you?"

He nodded furiously in reply. The New Queen considered questioning his table manners but was distracted when she saw a female Munchkin. She was only four feet tall and was wearing a blue dress.

"Is blue the color of your people?" the New Queen asked, staring at her coldly.

Caught off guard, the Munchkin blurted out the best thing she could come up with, "Not anymore. We're changing to red!"

The New Queen responded with an unconvincing chuckle.

The only person at the table that she could not find issue with was the pretty Quadling girl. She sat so quietly in her red dress that the New Queen hadn't noticed her while criticizing the rest of her tablemates. But then the Quadling's ruby bracelet had caught her attention.

"That's a pretty bracelet, may I have it?" she asked.

The Quadling quickly pulled her hand out of sight.

The New Queen had an inkling that something was afoot. Instead of forcing her to give up the bracelet, she asked once more, "May I have that lovely bracelet?"

The Quadling wasn't sure how to respond. Everyone at the table watched closely, their eyes darting from the New Queen to the Quadling while unthinkingly clutching items of their own. Almost immediately, the New Queen knew what was going on. There was no longer any reason to play nice.

Pointing her finger at the unsuspecting Nome, whose hands were wrapped around a jewel on his vest, she used her magic to lift him from his seat high above the ground. Everyone gasped in horror; they knew what would happen next. Desperate cries rose from the table.

"What were you all planning to do?" the New Queen demanded, ignoring their terrified pleas.

"Nothing, Your Highness! Nothing!" the Munchkin quickly replied.

"I don't believe you," she said, and abruptly stopped the flow of magic on the Nome. The unfortunate Nome fell to the ground with a loud crack and didn't get up after that. Screams immediately echoed in the courtyard, but fear kept everyone in their seats.

"Bring me his jewel!" the New Queen ordered.

When her guards brought the translucent brown jewel to her, she pressed her diamond to its surface. The jewel turned to stone, then crumbled into dust.

Turning back to the table, she pointed at the Quadling and again asked in a scarily gentle tone, "May I have that bracelet?"

There was no hesitation this time as the Quadling clumsily removed the ruby bracelet and placed it in front of the New Queen. Everyone at the table followed suit. The Wheeler took off his belt, the Munchkin took off her earrings, and the Gillikin took off his watch. They placed the items before the queen, and one by one she absorbed each item's magic with her diamond ring.

When all that was left was dust, the New Queen rose to her feet and announced, "Magic is prohibited throughout Oz. Those who are caught using it will die a horrible death!"

The response to the new decree was silence. As far as she was concerned, silence was consent.

As the macabre celebration continued, an uninvited creature found its way into the dungeons of Emerald City. The tiny fairy with large green wings fluttered toward a floating cage. She was invisible, but she could become visible to whomever she chose. That night, she chose the old witch Glinda.

Glinda was locked in a square cage wrapped with thorny, dark-green vines. When she saw the fairy, she gripped the bars and said, "Stop." There was urgency in her weak voice.

The fairy abruptly halted her fluttering wings and landed on one of the bars of the cage. She looked at Glinda questioningly.

As though she was able to read her mind, Glinda said softly, "You can't save me. This magic is too strong."

"Then what can I do?" the fairy asked in a squeaky, worried voice.

Glinda remained silent for a few seconds to gather her strength before she said, "I need you to do something for me."

"What?" the fairy asked.

"I need you to bring Dorothy back."

CHAPTER 5

The tiny fairy fluttered out of the dark dungeon, unsure what to do next. Glinda had had to stop talking when the feathered guards had appeared, and the tiny fairy had left without further instructions. Feathered guards had a way of smelling fairies and then catching them in their beaks.

The tiny fairy flew out into the night sky. Perched on the New Queen's statue, she watched for a while how the terrified citizens forced down their dinner. She noticed the empty seat at the New Queen's table and wondered where the Nome had gone. Imagining the worst, she spread her wings and left Emerald City.

The night was cold and windy, so even just a few minutes of flying took so much of her strength that she slumped on a tree branch the moment she had the chance. She didn't know what to do. All she could think about was returning home. But she couldn't give up. Propping herself against the tree, she tried to recall her memories of Dorothy.

It was not that long ago that Dorothy had come to Oz and defeated the Wicked Witch of the West. The fairy recalled she'd had friends with her, and with that memory she leapt back into the air. She knew who she should see. He always wore a high-crowned, wide-brimmed hat and carried a leather-bound book. It was none other than Scarecrow.

After Dorothy had left Oz, all her friends had gone their separate ways. Tin Woodman became the emperor of the Winkies, and Brave Lion, a chief guard in Emerald City, had left on a mission before the arrival of the New Queen and not been seen since. Scarecrow was said to be traveling the world for more knowledge. But the tiny fairy knew better. On occasion she'd relayed messages from Glinda to Scarecrow, and she was certain he hadn't left his castle in the woods.

Spreading her wings, the tiny fairy embarked on her journey. Scarecrow's castle wasn't big, nor was it intact. It had been abandoned many years ago, and parts of it had collapsed. Scarecrow lived in one of the towers, where he read his books and studied ancient magic day and night. He only left in the early evening to go for a walk in the woods and was always back in his tower by nightfall. It is true that he had once traveled the world, but after collecting all his books, he'd put his traveling days behind him and retired to reading.

When the tiny fairy arrived at the castle, the sun was just rising. Seeing that the day was about to break, she wasted no time and headed straight to Scarecrow's tower, where she found him resting, his eyes closed, with an open book on his chest.

"Scarecrow!" she shouted as she flew toward him. "Scarecrow, wake up!"

Scarecrow groggily opened his eyes and shot straight up in his chair.

"Tiny fairy, what are you doing here?" he asked.

"Glinda needs your help," the tiny fairy replied.

"I am always at her assistance," he said, taking off his hat with a nod.

"She needs you to bring Dorothy back to Oz."

"Why?" Scarecrow raised an eyebrow.

"Haven't you heard? Oz has a new queen, and she is wicked!"

"Like the Wicked Witch of the West?"

"No, Scarecrow. She's worse! How do you not know this?" the tiny fairy asked in surprise.

"I don't get out a lot." Scarecrow paused and silently scolded himself for locking himself away. "But I can bring Dorothy back."

The tiny fairy clapped in glee and watched him get to work. Without needing to refer to any of the books on his messy table, he pulled open a drawer and retrieved a torn piece of blue cloth.

Then turning to the fairy, he asked, "Do you have white fairy dust?"

The tiny fairy nodded and blew on her palm. Scarecrow grabbed an empty wooden bowl to collect the glittering white flakes that flew at him. Then he set the blue cloth on fire and threw it into the bowl. When the fire died out, he mixed the ashes and poured them into a little pouch.

"Let's take a walk, shall we?" Scarecrow said as he pocketed the pouch.

They walked to an open field where there was no one around. It seemed to be a safe spot to do magic. Placing the pouch on the grass, Scarecrow backed away as far as he could. When the pouch was barely still in sight, he pulled out a matchbox, lit a match, and decisively flicked it in the pouch's direction. The tiny fairy could only wonder if that was the best way to set it on fire.

. . .

It was the perfect day to spend outside, and Dorothy was fully enjoying it. After an early breakfast, she grabbed a book and went out to the field with her dog, Toto. Toto happily dashed about as she lay on her stomach, settling in for a good read. When Toto had had enough running around, he sat right next to Dorothy as she read aloud.

Just as the story was picking up pace, Toto got to his feet and began to bark at the sky. Looking up at the dark clouds, Dorothy knew something wasn't right. She watched a swirl of wind drop from the clouds to the grass a few feet away from her. Her first instinct was to run. She dropped her book and ran away with all her might. But when she looked over her shoulder, she saw Toto glued to the spot, barking.

Dorothy had no choice but to run back. The moment she picked him up, she felt the strong wind suck her in. There was no point in fighting a tornado. All she could do was scream.

Seconds later, Dorothy was thrown forward onto soft green grass. She was completely confused about what had just happened, but before she could make sense of anything, Toto slipped from her grasp and ran away from her, barking happily.

"Toto!" Dorothy called as she looked up. To her shock, she felt a rush of joy.

Her good friend Scarecrow was offering his hand to help her up. With a big smile on his face, he tipped his hat and said, "Welcome back, Dorothy. You've grown!"

"More than you had expected?" Dorothy asked with a cheeky smile.

"Way more! I was expecting to see a child, not an adult."

She simply laughed in response.

It was a sweet moment of reunion between the two as Toto excitedly jumped on them. But they didn't realize that a feathered guard had seen the tornado—birds could easily see it from miles away.

The guard ran to the New Queen's chamber and hastily knocked on the door. It was only because he wanted to keep his head that he didn't run in.

When she didn't open the door, he shouted, "Your Highness, I saw a tornado like the one that brought us here! Someone has done magic!"

A few seconds later, the door swung open, and the New Queen stared him down. "Not just magic—someone has arrived! Find out who."

CHAPTER 6

Scarecrow brought Dorothy back to his little hideout while the tiny fairy carried the news of Dorothy's return to Glinda. Dorothy sensed something bad had happened when Scarecrow sent the fairy on her way, but she remained silent. She guessed it was probably the reason for her return. The thought bothered her, but she ignored it while she caught up with her old friend.

When they finally climbed up the long spiral staircase, Scarecrow ushered Dorothy into his small home and quickly cleared a chair stacked with books.

"It's a little messy, I know. I haven't had time to organize everything," he said.

"Reading does take a lot of time," Dorothy replied with a smile.

Toto, who was previously so full of energy, now rested his head on his paws as Scarecrow rooted through a drawer for a dog treat.

"So, tell me, Scarecrow, what has happened to Oz?" Dorothy asked.

He sighed and leaned against a wooden table. "I don't know much, because I haven't been out a lot. But the tiny fairy told me an evil queen has taken over, and Glinda asked her to bring you back."

"Where is Glinda?"

"Most likely in a lot of trouble."

"Then I need to save her," she said and got to her feet.

"Hold on, we don't know what the situation is like in Emerald City. And let's not forget that you don't have any weapons," he said.

Dorothy looked worried for a few seconds, then smiled. She knew Scarecrow well enough to know he'd probably kept her weapons.

"Where are they?" she asked quickly.

"Now, now. Who says I'm going to give them to you? I can't let you go running off to Emerald City and get yourself killed."

"I'm not stupid, Scarecrow. But I need my weapons."

He thought for a while, but although it was against his better judgment, he eventually gave in.

"Fine, but you'll do as I say until we hear from Glinda."

Dorothy nodded and let Scarecrow take the lead. Toto did not seem remotely interested in the retrieval of her weapons, so they left him lying on the rug. As they descended the spiral staircase, she was tempted to ask him where he'd hidden them, but she soon decided it was more exciting if she didn't know. So Dorothy kept the question to herself as they walked through a courtyard overgrown with weeds and headed down another flight of stairs.

When it grew too dark to see in the stairwell, Scarecrow pulled out his matchbox and lit a match. He flicked it down the steps and said, "Not much farther. Watch your step."

The stairs ended on a dark landing. The air was wet and cold, and it sent shivers down Dorothy's spine. Scarecrow lit another match and used it to light the torch he took from the damp, musty brick wall.

"Follow me closely. It is easy to get lost down here," he said, his words echoing down the dark tunnel.

The torch burned surprisingly long as the two of them turned corners, descended more steps, and made their way deeper into the darkness. When curiosity finally took over, Dorothy asked, "What is this place?"

"This is an underground passageway that leads to the neighboring towns. Since the castle was destroyed, nobody uses it. They say if you listen carefully, you can hear the cries of the dead."

"I don't believe you," Dorothy said, and just then she felt the hair on the back of her neck raise. She didn't tell Scarecrow, of course—he would have laughed at her.

Not long after that hair-raising moment, they entered a circular chamber. Scarecrow lit several torches on the wall, and the darkness fled. The wall was damp, the floor was cracked, and there was a puddle of water in the middle. Droplets of water fell from the ceiling and plopped into the puddle, joining the others.

Dorothy followed Scarecrow as he approached the puddle. The floor tilted slightly toward the center, and she felt like she could easily fall on the slippery floor.

"Don't come too close, Dorothy," Scarecrow said as he knelt on one knee. Although the puddle looked shallow, she couldn't see the bottom of it.

"I won't fall in," she said as she watched him pick up a rusty chain that trailed into the water.

"I'm not afraid of you falling, I'm afraid you'll be pulled in," Scarecrow replied and began to pull the chain.

"What do you mean by that?"

"It's best you don't know," he said.

Dorothy didn't question him further as he pulled the chain from the apparently deep puddle. As he reached the end of the chain, a chest peeked out of the water. She stepped forward to give Scarecrow a hand.

"Don't!" he snapped.

His voice bounced off the chamber's walls, and Dorothy heard a flapping of wings.

"Did you hear that?" she asked.

Another tunnel was connected to the chamber, but darkness had swallowed it whole. Dorothy stared into it intensely, hoping to see a bird, but gave up when Scarecrow dragged the chest out of the water and laid it at her feet.

Looking down, she saw a square chest wrapped with chains. A lock held the rusted metal together. Scarecrow unlocked it with a key from his pocket and freed the chest from its metal binds. Dorothy quickly opened it.

"There's no rush," Scarecrow said.

But Dorothy was not in a hurry because she was excited—she actually felt extremely uneasy. She sensed that something was watching them, although she could not see what. Pushing her fear briefly aside, she focused on the items in the chest.

There were two sacks: one about the size of her palm, and the other the size of a fat book. Opening the bigger sack, Dorothy found her trusted whip. Its handle and long, tough leather were still in good shape. Moving on to the next sack, she found it filled with cookies and candy. Each piece was colorfully wrapped and labeled differently.

"I bet you can't find candy like that anywhere else, eh?" Scarecrow said with a chuckle.

"Oh yes, no such flavors at home," Dorothy replied as she hung the smaller sack and her whip from the adjustable belts on the sides of her fitted blue vest.

"Ready to go?" Scarecrow asked.

"Let's get out of here," she said.

As they began to retrace their steps, Dorothy took one last look into the dark tunnel. Seeing nothing, she convinced herself the sound had been just her imagination.

She was wrong, of course. The bird whose flapping wings had echoed down the tunnel slipped out into the neighboring town. It was a raven unlike any other, with strange markings on its feathers. It flew straight to Emerald City, its destination the New Queen's windowsill.

When the New Queen saw it, she let it come inside her room. It immediately spread its wings and transformed into one of her guards.

"This magic is powerful indeed," she said, rubbing the diamond on her finger.

"It is, Your Highness," the guard replied with a bow.

"Now, tell me, who is this intruder?"

"Her name is Dorothy. She is with a man. He gave her a whip and a sack of candy," the guard reported.

"A sack of candy?"

"Yes, Your Highness."

"Must have a sweet tooth." The New Queen paused to sit down before continuing." Catch this Dorothy and bring her to me. I want to see how sweet she is."

CHAPTER 7

Dorothy felt her uneasiness finally lift from her chest when they entered Scarecrow's home. She felt so much safer in the cluttered room. When Toto hurried to her side, her worries vanished entirely.

Toto had a very good nose, so Dorothy knew he could smell the cookies and candy. She pulled out a special treat for him from the sack. The cookie was shaped like a bone, and a label on its wrapper read Toto. It was a cookie only for him. When she fed it to him, he chomped down on it in a hurry. Once he'd licked up all the crumbs on the floor, Toto obediently sat at Dorothy's side. He knew very well not to ask for another—when it came to this kind of cookie, one was enough.

"We should wait for the tiny fairy before we do anything else," Scarecrow said and sat in an old worn-out armchair.

Dorothy nodded in reply. She wanted to save Glinda but knew it was wiser to wait for her orders. Oz was now unknown territory, and something felt very wrong. Even though she knew so little about the current state of this world, she could sense the danger.

When evening arrived and the tiny fairy still had not returned, Scarecrow offered Dorothy and Toto some fruit. He apologized for the lack of food, but Dorothy didn't blame him. He was a scarecrow, after all, and didn't need to eat.

After his two visitors filled their bellies, Scarecrow made his bed for Dorothy and told her to rest. It wasn't easy for her to fall asleep, but after a few hours of watching the lit candles melt and Scarecrow read his books, Dorothy shut her eyes and did not open them again till morning.

. . .

As the sun dawned the following day, it did not arrive alone. At first, Dorothy thought she was dreaming. The sound of feet stomping and Toto's barking, all fused into a horrible rhythm. But when her eyes shot open, she immediately knew it was no dream.

Toto was barking loudly, and Scarecrow had just woken up to the sound as well. He hurried to a window to figure out what was happening and panicked at what he saw.

"Oh no, this is not good," he said.

"What is it?" Dorothy quickly asked.

"We need to go," he replied.

He swiftly grabbed a leather-bound book and headed for the door. Dorothy paused to look out the window, but he waved her over in a hurry.

"What's going on?" she asked as they hurried down the steps. Toto had taken the lead and soon disappeared ahead of them.

"There are soldiers below, soldiers I've never seen before. This is bad."

"How many are there?"

"Many."

Dorothy unhooked her whip from her vest, ready to defend herself. As they neared the bottom of the tower, they heard Toto barking and growling. They didn't need to question who he was barking at—they were soon surrounded by bird-like soldiers.

"Dorothy, the New Queen has ordered your arrest," one of the soldiers said.

She didn't know how they knew her name, but she did know she was in big trouble. Releasing her whip, Dorothy said, "I don't think so."

Toto made the first move and leapt onto a soldier's chest, biting down on his beak. The soldier yanked him off and threw him against a wall. Dorothy heard a loud thud followed by an angry growl. Maybe she'd given Toto the cookie too soon, because his eyes were turning from black to red.

"No, Toto! Run!" Dorothy cried. She did not want them to know what Toto could do, especially if they were in a losing battle.

Toto hesitated, but when Dorothy repeated the order, the little dog ran. He took off in the opposite direction and disappeared through a crack in a wall.

With Toto out of sight, Dorothy swung her whip at a soldier. It looped around his neck, and when she pulled he fell forward. She then slashed at three soldiers, cutting through their feathers and leaving thin, sharp cuts on their cheeks. As she attempted another swing, one of them caught her whip and yanked on it. He was unexpectedly strong, and she sprawled on the ground.

Dorothy propped herself up and found that a dozen blades were pointed at her. She also saw Scarecrow with his hands up in surrender. It was too bad he knew how magic worked but wasn't able to do any tricks himself.

The soldiers wasted no time tying their wrists with rope and throwing them into a cage pulled behind a horse. They also took her whip and sack of candy, along with Scarecrow's magic book.

As the horse started to pull them down the bumpy road, Scarecrow whispered, "Where's Toto?"

Dorothy looked up at the sky, then with a small, tight smile, she said, "Right above us."

Scarecrow didn't have to look up, because he saw the shadow of a bird flying across the bottom of the cage. Toto was now a bird, free and by their side.

When they passed through the gates of Emerald City, Dorothy and Scarecrow finally saw the changes they'd heard about. The citizens quickly made way for the cage pulled through the streets. They said nothing but watched with pleading eyes. They knew who Dorothy was, and their expressions showed a mixture of fear and hope. She wanted to reassure them that everything would be all right, but she bit her tongue at the thought of putting them in danger.

When they reached the palace, Dorothy and Scarecrow were separated. Scarecrow was taken straight to the dungeons, while Dorothy was brought to the great hall. There, she found herself face-to-face with the New Queen.

She was seated on a giant gold-and-red throne with two muttbits by her side. Dorothy took in the ugly creatures, the New Queen's sly smile, and the massive changes to the great hall. Big lanterns hung from the ceiling, a giant rose was painted on the marble floor, and the pillars were wrapped with red silk.

"Welcome to the new Oz, Dorothy," the New Queen said.

"I prefer the old one," she boldly replied.

The New Queen gave a fake laugh and asked, "Really? It was too green for my liking."

"Oz is not yours to decide."

"It is mine now," she said with a shrug.

"What have you done to Queen Ozma and Glinda?" Dorothy demanded as they locked eyes.

Feeling not at all threatened, the New Queen got up from her throne and walked toward Dorothy, still keeping eye contact. "I'll tell you if you tell me one thing."

"What?"

"Where are you from?"

Dorothy wondered at the strange question but didn't hesitate to reply.

"I'm from Earth."

At hearing the name of Dorothy's home, the New Queen's eyes widened. She tried to suppress her hatred for the place but failed.

"Get this earthling out of my sight!" she ordered.

"Wait, you haven't answered me!" Dorothy shouted as the soldiers grabbed her by the arms.

"You'll find out soon enough," the New Queen replied.

Dorothy tried desperately to free herself from the soldiers' strong grip. As they dragged her down to the dungeons, all she could think about was the New Queen's reaction when she told her she was from Earth. *Why does she hate it?* Dorothy wondered. *And why is she afraid?*

CHAPTER 8

The dungeon had a low ceiling and two long rows of cells that faced each other. Almost all of them were empty, except for the ones at the far end. The farthest cell was also the biggest and faced the long walkway.

In that cell was a floating cage wrapped in thorns, but the dim light of the flickering torches made it hard for Dorothy to see who was in it. Only when she was thrown into the cell next to it did she recognize the figure.

"Glinda!" Dorothy called in shock. "Glinda, are you all right?"

"She's fine," Scarecrow replied from the cell across from Dorothy's.

She was relieved to see him, but the sight of Glinda locked up in such a horrible cage was troubling.

"Why is she locked up? Where is Queen Ozma?" Dorothy quickly asked.

"The thorns are meant to weaken her," Scarecrow answered her first question.

"I . . . do not know where Queen Ozma is," Glinda answered the second. The strain in her voice was not because of old age.

"We need to get out of here," Dorothy said. Weighing her options, she thought of the tiny fairy. "Glinda, where's the tiny fairy? Didn't she come to see you?"

There was a short moment of silence. Scarecrow answered on Glinda's behalf, "She never came."

"She never came?" Dorothy repeated. She could only imagine the worst.

A wave of uneasiness swept over her as she pictured all the possible reasons for the tiny fairy's disappearance. The New Queen clearly had a very strong grip on Oz, and Dorothy was afraid she could not fight her. At that moment, all she wanted to do was escape.

Pushing the tiny fairy from her thoughts, Dorothy looked around her cell for something she could use to get free. When she found nothing, she knelt by the lock to examine it.

"Dorothy, where's Toto?" Scarecrow asked.

The question shifted her focus, and she felt fearful again. "Isn't he with you?"

"No," he answered, then added, "don't worry. Toto is a smart dog, he'll be all right."

Not worrying was easier said than done. Dorothy gave him a reassuring nod, but she silently scolded herself for not looking out for Toto. She knew he was smart, and his special ability would protect him, but she could not shake off the heaviness in her chest. All she could do was hope for his return.

When night arrived, Toto still had not made an appearance, and Glinda hadn't said another word. She was probably too weak and tired to talk. Dorothy hesitated to ask her advice. What would they do now? How could they escape? Scarecrow had no ideas, and Dorothy was just as clueless.

All that thinking must have tired Dorothy out, because she found herself drifting off into a dream world. Her imagination collided with her worries to form strange images in her head. One of them was Toto's curious-looking face. When Dorothy did not respond to him, he licked her until she finally wiped her face and gently pushed him away. She then realized she wasn't dreaming—Toto was right next to her, looking up at her.

Dorothy felt so relieved. When she reached out for him to be sure she wasn't dreaming, he leapt off the prison cot and picked up a shiny, thin piece of metal from the ground and brought it to her. She knew immediately how to use it. Toto was smart indeed, and Dorothy gave him a quick kiss.

She stood up and whispered Scarecrow's name.

He hadn't slept the entire night, so when he heard his name, he hurried to the bars of his cell.

"This will get us out." Dorothy showed him the metal piece.

Just as Scarecrow responded with a thumbs-up, Glinda finally spoke. Her voice was soft, but her message was clear—it was the clearest "No" Dorothy had ever heard.

"Why?" Dorothy asked.

"Go, but we must stay," Glinda said.

"No, I won't leave you two behind."

"She's right, Dorothy. You can escape more easily by yourself," Scarecrow said.

"But I need you two. I wouldn't know what to do." Dorothy turned to Glinda for an answer.

"There is a book in my secret library. It will tell you," Glinda said. Her voice sounded stronger. Dorothy waited for her instructions.

"Listen carefully, Dorothy. Above the fireplace in my chamber, there's an orb. Turn it south, and it will reveal a passageway. That passageway will lead you to my secret library."

Glinda took a deep breath and shut her eyes. The few seconds of silence felt like hours, but neither Dorothy nor Scarecrow said a word. Even Toto didn't make a sound.

With her eyes still closed, Glinda continued, "The book you need is the twelfth book on the top row of the second bookshelf.

It will give you all the answers. And if you need anything else, my library has it."

At that moment Dorothy didn't know what else she would need, but Glinda's instructions were clear. She was glad to have at least that.

"I understand," she finally said. Glinda was right; she was better off alone.

Quickly, Dorothy began to pick the lock of her cell. After a few attempts, the lock clicked and the door swung open. She had learned how to pick locks back home, because she always misplaced her keys. That skill had now proven useful.

Hurrying to Scarecrow's cell, Dorothy said, "I'm worried they might hurt you."

"Don't worry about me. We'll both be fine," he assured her. He then reached into his pocket, pulled out his matchbox, and handed it to Dorothy. "You'll need this. Be careful, all right?"

Dorothy nodded and promised, "I'll return for both of you."

As she and Toto quietly walked down the empty walkway, she replayed Glinda's words in her head. She could not afford to forget them. By the time they reached the exit, Dorothy had them burned in her memory.

"Now, Toto. Do your thing," Dorothy whispered, and Toto disappeared around the corner. This time, she knew where he'd be. There was nothing to worry about. Toto was a smart dog, after all.

CHAPTER 9

Her body flattened against the wall, Dorothy strained her ears for her cue. She was counting on Toto but did not know what he'd planned. It was not the first time she had fully counted on her dog.

A few seconds after Toto had disappeared down the corner, she heard a bark and a jingle of keys.

"He's got the keys!" a guard shouted.

Dorothy heard heavy footsteps running and peeked around the corner to see if the coast was clear. The hallway forked—the shouting echoed down the left side, so she headed to the right. There were only a few torches lit, and the hallway was rather dim. Dorothy cautiously walked in the shadows. There was a flight of stairs leading up at the end of the corridor, and to the right of the staircase was a door.

Light seeped through the gaps in the doorway, and Dorothy inched closer to take a look. Through the keyhole she saw a guard sitting at a table. Her weapons were on a shelf. Just when she thought she needed Toto's help, the happy dog ran up to her.

"Good boy!" Dorothy whispered. "Now, I need you to take that guard out."

Toto wagged his tail in response. Dorothy opened the door as quietly as possible. When the gap was wide enough to fit a fat snake, Toto's body transformed. In the blink of an eye, his warm, furry body became cold and scaly. He slithered into the room and came back just as quickly. He then returned to his normal form, his tail wagging even faster than before.

"Good job, Toto," Dorothy said as she entered the room.

The guard's feathered face was flat on the table, and he didn't move when Dorothy touched him. Without wasting any time, she retrieved her whip and sack. She then poured out the contents of the sack on the table and read all the labels. When she found the one she was looking for, she returned the rest to the bag in a hurry. The other guards could walk in at any moment, and she did not want to be caught.

Dorothy popped a purplish, thumb-sized candy into her mouth, chewed, and swallowed. It tasted sweet. She stuffed the wrapper, which read CAMOUFLAGE, into her pocket before reaching for the lifeless guard again. Almost immediately, a purplish glow traveled from her finger and swept across her body. She didn't see any changes but knew the candy had worked—the candy and cookies from her sack always worked.

Dorothy and Toto left the room and climbed the stairs, which exited onto another hallway. The palace would have been a maze if she hadn't been there before, but with her memories and Toto's sense of direction, they knew exactly where they were going. The hallway led to the guards' quarters, which were connected to the palace by a courtyard. It did not take them long to reach the quarters, where Dorothy spotted two feathered guards lingering.

"Toto, go small," she whispered.

Toto did as he was told and shrunk into a rat. She picked him up and put him in her pocket before she approached the guards. As she drew near, her heart began to race. She was well aware that she was camouflaged, but that didn't make it easier.

"Going for a stroll?" one of the guards asked her.

"I wish," Dorothy simply replied, hoping she played her character well.

"Must be boring down there. It's not like the prisoners can escape," another guard said.

"Tell that to the queen. I could die just sitting all day," Dorothy said.

"At least that's better than having your head chopped off," the first guard said. His friend chuckled nervously.

"I agree. I better get going before I lose mine. Her Highness has summoned me," Dorothy lied convincingly.

"I bet she wants that earthling executed. They're always causing problems," he continued.

Dorothy wanted to leave, but what he said made her linger.

"She seems pretty harmless though, unlike you-know-who," the other guard added.

"You-know-who?" Dorothy couldn't help asking.

"Oh, come on, I'm not saying her name. If Her Highness hears it, she'll go crazy!"

"You're right. Well, I better get going," Dorothy quickly replied.

She hadn't learned much from the two guards, but she did now know that the New Queen was afraid of another earthling. Dorothy hoped to find out who the mysterious person was when she got to Glinda's secret library.

As she entered the palace, she trusted her instincts and headed straight to the second floor. The palace had been redecorated so that all the hallways looked the same, and she had to rely on her memory to find her way. Thankfully, the changes to the walls and floors didn't lead her down the wrong path.

Dorothy slipped through the white doors to Glinda's chamber and pushed a heavy armchair behind them. Turning around, she was in for a shock—the pages of Glinda's books were ripped, the mirrors were broken, and the bed was torn. Glancing around the room, Dorothy spotted the fireplace where Glinda said she'd find the orb. It was to the side, away from the mess.

Watching where she stepped, Dorothy headed toward it. She stopped in her tracks when she saw herself in a broken piece of mirror. Staring at the guard in her reflection, she saw the veil beginning to drop and her true self show. Dorothy was no longer in disguise. She could not afford to get caught now; she had made it this far. She prayed the evil magic in Oz would not stand in her way.

Once Dorothy reached the fireplace, she took Toto from her pocket, and he returned to his original tail-wagging form. When she found the orb, her jaw dropped. A globe depicting Oz, it was stuck in the wall above the fireplace. It did not look like something that could be moved, and it was out of her reach even if it could be. Glinda would have had no problem turning the orb south with her wand, but Dorothy had nothing to aid her.

Racking her brain for a solution, she didn't realize she was in danger until Toto barked softly. She stopped to listen and heard voices outside the door. She knew what to do. There was no time to make out what they were saying. She picked Toto up and placed him on top of the fireplace.

"Spin the orb, Toto," Dorothy ordered.

Toto rested his paws on the orb and pushed down on it. The orb rotated 270 degrees before it locked into place at six o'clock and began to glow. The fireplace started to move sideways. When there was enough space for them to enter, Dorothy grabbed a candlestick from a nearby table and slipped through.

As soon as they entered the darkness, Dorothy felt the walls for a switch that would close the fireplace. When she found one, she did not hesitate to pull the lever. The fireplace shut tightly behind them, silencing the world on the other side. Dorothy could only hope the New Queen's guards didn't see that.

She was glad she had Scarecrow's matchbox. After the match's little flame brought the candle to life, Dorothy found herself standing before a flight of descending steps. She couldn't see how far she had to go, but she knew she was going in the right direction. Taking a deep breath, she began her descent into darkness. Hopefully, whatever revelation they found below would be brighter than the light from their candle.

CHAPTER 10

Darkness has a way of making the shortest journey feel the longest. As they stepped slowly and carefully down the stairs, Dorothy could not help but glance quickly behind them. Even though she could no longer see the outline of the fireplace, she felt safer checking.

When they finally reached the end of the staircase, they found themselves in front of a wooden door. Thankfully, the door was unlocked. It opened into a dark room. Dorothy couldn't tell how big the room was or what was in it. She could only see a wall in the light of her candle, and to her surprise that was enough. She found one torch, then another without any trouble. Soon, the darkness dissipated, and Dorothy could take a good look around.

The room was neither big nor small. There were two bookshelves facing the door with a long table and chairs between them. Dorothy set the candle down and recalled what Glinda had told her.

"The twelfth book on the top row of the second bookshelf," she muttered to herself.

She walked up to the bookshelf on her right. Looking up at the top row, she began to count. Stopping on the twelfth book, she had to pull the book out on tiptoe. It had a brown cover without a title. The pages were uneven and some of them stuck out.

Dorothy blew the dust off the cover and sneezed. There was no doubt that this book had sat untouched for many years, and she was amazed that Glinda could remember its contents despite having so many other books around.

Dorothy took a seat. Toto leapt onto the table and gave the book a sniff. When she didn't make a move to open the book, Toto barked softly. She was nervous about its contents. The weight on her shoulders felt too heavy to bear. The responsibility of saving Oz was now on her, and she feared she might fail. Toto, however, thought differently. He used his paw to flip the cover open. When her eyes fell on the first page, she pushed her fear aside as excitement and curiosity took over.

The book was written in slanting black letters. Different types of materials and small items were stuck to the pages, as well as drawings of creatures, objects, and people that Dorothy didn't recognize. It was basically a traveler's journal about another world, filled with everything she needed to know. More importantly, it was the answer to saving Oz.

Flipping through the pages, Dorothy learned about this other world, so different from Earth and Oz. There were creatures and unique, colorful plants she had never seen before. As she went deeper into the book, she met a young girl named Alice who had entered that land. She was also from Earth and only a child when she first met the Queen of Hearts. Alice bravely stood up to her and almost had her head chopped off. She didn't stop fighting, even after escaping death on several occasions, and convinced the people of Wonderland to fight against the queen too.

It was a battle for power, but nothing good ultimately came of it. The Queen of Hearts managed to overpower her people, and Alice was forced to leave. But they hadn't been completely defeated, or so the author of this journal thought. Whoever he was, he ended the book with a note that read, "Alice left a message: the Queen of Hearts will not rule forever."

The Queen of Hearts looked exactly like the New Queen of Oz. Dorothy gave the author credit for both art and prophecy. Even though he wasn't entirely spot on—the Queen of Hearts had found a new land to rule after Alice left—he believed she could be defeated. After reading the journal, Dorothy knew what she should do next. It was a crazy idea, but it was the only one she had.

Dorothy had no idea how old the book was, or how old Alice would be now. All she had was a piece of Alice's dress to help locate her. She was certain that Alice was no longer a child, but hopefully she was still strong enough to fight alongside her. The only thing Dorothy still needed to carry out her plan was some fairy dust.

"Where can I find black fairy dust, Toto?" she asked softly, not really hoping for an answer.

Toto responded to her question by jumping onto a chair and clawing the edge of the table. Dorothy attempted to stop him, then realized the table was thicker than a typical one of its size. Glinda's words shot to mind: "If you need anything else, my library has it." She ran her hand under the table, feeling for something. She walked along the length of the table, concentrating on her sense of touch, and came across a small button. She pushed it, and a large drawer on the opposite side of the table popped open. It contained a bottle filled with black fairy dust and a few empty pouches. There were also small pieces of parchment and a type of cloth one typically found in Oz.

Without thinking twice, Dorothy prepared for her next move. She poured black fairy dust into two pouches and added materials from Oz she burned in a small bowl to make the powdery mixture complete. Then she made another pouch for her journey back to Earth with the piece of Alice's dress. She also filled a larger pouch with the remaining fairy dust—she had a feeling she would need it later, and even if she didn't, she would rather play it safe.

When she was done, Dorothy cleared an area in the middle of the library and placed the pouch with the ashes of Alice's dress on the floor. Taking a few steps back, she pulled out Scarecrow's matchbox and lit a match. Throwing it on the pouch, Dorothy hoped the fire wouldn't cause a tornado. She didn't want to destroy the secret library—or see Glinda's horror if she did.

The small flame set the pouch on fire. Shortly after the flames fizzled out, the ground below it sunk in, and a large bottomless rabbit hole appeared. Not being able to see the bottom was a little terrifying, but she was in no position to be afraid. Grabbing Toto and the book on Wonderland, Dorothy ignored her fears and jumped.

CHAPTER 11

Down and down she went. Hugging the book and Toto tight to her chest, Dorothy anticipated a painful landing. Surprisingly, when she finally landed in a heap, it wasn't—but there was a horrid stench in the air that made her gag.

It was too dark to see where she was, but Scarecrow's matchbox came to the rescue. Once she'd finally lit a match, everything made sense. Dorothy was in an underground sewer, and right above her head was the exit. Not waiting for rats to scurry over her feet, she climbed up the ladder and pushed the manhole cover aside. Light flooded in like a spotlight. Dorothy wasted no time and helped Toto out before pulling herself up.

Away from the stench, Dorothy found herself in a narrow alley. Looking up at the sky, she saw tall chimneys reaching for the clouds. They puffed out black smoke, and she could clearly hear the sound of machinery. Having taken in her surroundings, she didn't stick around.

Dorothy headed toward the street at the end of the alley. But as she drew near it, she hesitated. The people in the wet, dirty streets of this industrial town looked different and spoke in a foreign language. She didn't know which Asian country she was in, but she definitely didn't fit in. She also wasn't sure if it was wise to go looking for Alice.

As she hesitated, Dorothy spotted a few men in European clothing. It looked like they were trying to do business without attracting any attention. Maybe if she acted natural, people wouldn't notice her. With that thought in mind, she clutched the book tighter and exited the alley.

Toto trotted happily along. He seemed to be enjoying himself, while Dorothy awkwardly stared straight ahead. Occasionally, she quickly glanced around for clues, but all she saw were people shouting at each other. She thought about asking for help, but nobody was paying any attention to her, which was both a blessing and a curse.

A few minutes later, Dorothy stood outside the entrance to a factory. She felt so lost that she had to fight the urge to return to Oz. The thought gripped her so tightly, it took Toto's barking to bring her back to the real world. When she finally acknowledged him, Toto ran up to the entrance and started scratching it.

"Stop that!" Dorothy scolded. "You're drawing attention to us."

Toto didn't listen and kept scratching. She had no choice but to pick him up. Toto then barked at something above the entrance. Looking up, Dorothy saw a sign written both in English and in a foreign language. It read GOLDEN DRAGON CLOTH FACTORY.

Cloth factory? Dorothy thought. Recalling the bit of dress material she had burned, she realized it was no ordinary cloth. It was smoother and softer than any fabric she'd felt before. Alice must be here. Toto barked as if to say "That's what I was trying to tell you!" and Dorothy kissed him in response. What would she do without him?

They entered the factory. It was rather large, with many different kinds of machines. Some were big and automated, while others were small and hand operated. Dorothy cautiously crept along, keeping an eye out for an office. Factories always had offices, or at least that was what her uncle had told her.

When she spotted the stairs leading to the second floor, she ignored the strange stares and hurried toward it. The workers whispered among themselves, but the machines drowned out their voices. When she finally reached the second floor, she found a door with a sign that read MANAGEMENT.

"This must be it," Dorothy said to Toto.

Knocking on the door, she hoped to find someone who could help her. Instead, an old lady brusquely waved her into the small, crowded office.

"Wait," the old lady told her.

"I'm looking for someone," Dorothy said.

"Wait," she repeated and showed Dorothy the chair.

"I just need to know if an Alice works here," Dorothy continued.

"Wait," the old lady said again.

That was probably all the English the old lady knew, so Dorothy stopped her attempts to communicate and took a seat. The old lady said something to a young girl seated at one of the desks. The girl then got to her feet and hurried out a door at the back of the office. All Dorothy could do now was wait and hope that the girl had been sent to find Alice.

After a few minutes, an older girl around Dorothy's age came in with the young girl. She had short black hair, and when she walked up to Dorothy, she had a small smile on her face.

"I'm afraid the circus has left town," she said when her eyes fell on Toto and the whip that hung at Dorothy's waist.

Dorothy quickly got to her feet and said, "No, no. I'm not looking for the circus. I'm looking for someone else."

"And who is it that you're looking for?"

"I think she works here. Her name is Alice," Dorothy answered, and Toto barked softly.

"Cute dog," the older girl replied. "But I don't think the person you're looking for works here."

"Oh, do you know of anyone named Alice, then?" She was not going to leave without some information about her.

"Maybe. May I know why you're looking for Alice?"

"Well . . ." Dorothy trailed off, unsure how much she should give away. Deciding to play it safe, she said, "I need her help."

"How can Alice help you? She's not very good with animals," the girl replied, clearly amused by the unexpected guest.

"It's hard to explain. I mean, only Alice will understand."

"If it's a dress, you don't need Alice to make it for you."

"No, it's not a dress. I need Alice to help . . ." Dorothy paused and contemplated what to say again. Would this girl think she's crazy?

"You need Alice to help . . . ?" the girl prompted.

"To help defeat the Queen of Hearts," Dorothy quickly said. She regretted it almost immediately and hoped the girl hadn't caught what she'd said.

"I see," the girl merely replied.

"Only Alice will understand," Dorothy said again.

"She understands, all right. Now, who are you?"

It took Dorothy a moment to decipher the girl's comment, but when she did, a light bulb went off.

"Wait, are you Alice?" she asked excitedly. "But I thought you said Alice, er, you don't work here?"

"I don't. This is my father's company. Now it's my turn to ask the questions. Who are you?"

"I'm Dorothy, and I come from Oz."

"Oz?"

"The Queen of Hearts's new home."

CHAPTER 12

Alice led Dorothy through the back door and down a narrow hallway. They stopped in front of a metal door just before reaching the corner. Alice pushed it open. It screeched, revealing a small metal balcony. When Alice slammed the door shut, the balcony vibrated, and Dorothy immediately grabbed onto the railing. She couldn't help but imagine falling.

"The screws are a little loose, so you might not want to lean on the railing," Alice said with the same small smile.

Dorothy nodded nervously in reply as Alice began to climb up a ladder on the brick wall. She couldn't wait to get off the balcony. Once Alice was on the roof, she quickly handed Toto and the book to her, then made her way up. Although she wasn't afraid of heights, she wasn't a big fan, either. The moment she set foot on the uneven cement, she hurried away from the edge. She was clearly different from Alice, who sat with her legs dangling off the edge, leaning forward to examine the journal. Dorothy would never do that.

"Where did you get this book?" Alice asked as she flipped through the traveler's journal.

"From a secret library," she answered. She would have explained further, but there was no time. "I need you to return to Oz with me."

"Return to Oz with you?" Alice repeated with a chuckle.

"Yes. Only you can defeat the Queen of Hearts."

"You've read this book, right?" She paused to wave the journal. "Then you'd know I didn't defeat her. I failed."

"You didn't fail. The only reason why the Queen of Hearts is in Oz is because she left Wonderland. Something must have happened there."

"Well, even so, what do you expect me to do?"

"She's afraid of you for some—"

"You want me to go to Oz and give her a scare?"

"I . . . Well, maybe that could help? I mean, there has to be a reason why I was sent to get you," Dorothy said, suddenly unsure what she was doing.

"So you don't know why you were sent here?" Alice asked in disbelief.

"All I know is that you can help us. You've defeated the Queen of Hearts before, and you can do it again."

"You have so much faith in me, and you don't even know me," Alice replied.

"Just come back to Oz and help me figure things out."

There was a short moment of silence as Dorothy waited for a response. When Alice didn't reply, the silence became awkward. Dorothy felt the urge to break it, but right before a word could escape her lips, Alice spoke.

"Do you know that this kind of talk could have us locked away in a nuthouse? The Westerners are quite influential here, and they've set up a few nuthouses along the way."

The change of topic caught Dorothy off guard, but she managed to say, "We're not crazy."

"Of course we're not. But I'm not going to follow you."

"But—But we need you, Alice. Oz is in—"

"I didn't say I wasn't going, I just said I won't be following," Alice interrupted.

"Oh," Dorothy muttered.

"Now, how do I get to Oz?"

Dorothy quickly pulled out the pouches she had prepared earlier and handed one to Alice. She explained how the magic worked and stressed that Alice find an open area before setting the pouch on fire. Alice merely nodded when Dorothy was done, and Dorothy couldn't help wondering if she'd understood her.

Alice said she needed a few hours before she could head to Oz and explained that there was a construction site nearby. The ground had just been dug up, and the workers left for the night. After listening to her, Dorothy and Toto parted ways with Alice. As night fell on the industrial town, they headed toward the construction site. It was strange to walk against the tired crowd, but she was too preoccupied to notice the looks she was getting.

"Do you think she will come, Toto?" Dorothy asked when they finally reached their destination.

Toto gave her a reassuring bark and trotted to the center of the dug-up soil. Finding comfort in her little companion's faith, Dorothy followed him and set the pouch down. Shortly after, a small tornado no one else noticed sent Dorothy back to Oz.

. . .

Alice sat on her bed with the pouch in her hand. The clanking and banging were absent at night. Her father was having their home renovated, so every day she escaped the noise by heading to his factory office. Who could have known this would be the day she finally had to confront her imagination?

There'd been nights when she'd wondered if Wonderland was just in her head, after all. Her mother said she had an overactive imagination, and her father was convinced it was just a phase. As the years went by, Alice had started to believe them, but the day's events raised questions.

The girl named Dorothy spoke convincingly about the Queen of Hearts. She also mentioned Wonderland and another world as well. Alice had never heard of Oz before, which made her wonder if Dorothy was part of her imagination too.

"At least the dog couldn't talk," Alice said to herself as she slumped on her bed. "And I was definitely not dreaming. Old Lady Lee saw her too."

Looking at the pouch in her hand, Alice decided to give it a try. If it was just her imagination, burning the pouch would have no effect. But if it worked . . . Well, then Alice would just have to save Oz.

She got up lazily from her bed and faced the wall beside her large wardrobe. When she'd returned from Wonderland many years ago, she'd hidden the items she'd brought home with her in the wall. It wasn't much, but they kept her sane. If it weren't for them, she would have admitted she was crazy long ago.

Pulling out a loose brick, Alice reached in and took out a small box. Inside the box were a small sack filled with dried rose petals and two playing cards. She was immediately flooded with memories of Hatter, the Queen of Hearts, and the world of Wonderland. She remembered its being rather similar to home but more ancient and magical, and without intending to, she began to miss it.

Stuffing the items into the pockets of her skirt, Alice retrieved a flintlock pistol, a few lead balls, and a bag of gunpowder from her desk. She also grabbed a matchbox.

"'Set fire only in an open area,' she said," Alice mused out loud as she looked at the pouch. "But the last time I came back from Wonderland, not a second ticked by. What damage can this do?"

Looking at the calendar on her desk, Alice took note of the date. It was September 29, 1938, and the clock on her table had just ticked eight.

"Well, my room is big enough," she said and placed the pouch on the marble floor. She then lit a match and knelt down to set the pouch on fire. Alice did not back away when the pouch began to burn, and she did not move an inch when the fire fizzled. She was so close to the pouch that when the wind burst from it, she was pulled in before she could even realize what was happening.

That day, there was no rabbit hole for Alice. There was just a very surprising tornado.

2
ADVENTUS

CHAPTER 13

No one saw the swirling wind that formed in the clouds of the night sky. It stretched and reached down between the trees, and when its tip touched the ground, it pulled back up immediately and disappeared, leaving a few broken branches and a girl sprawled on the forest floor.

As Alice opened her eyes, she noticed she was holding her breath. Was she in another world? She could have easily mistaken the forest for one back home, but the fact that she was just in her bedroom a few seconds ago told her this wasn't Earth. She couldn't believe what she saw.

Getting to her feet, Alice dusted off her skirt and looked up at the sky. The clouds glided by slowly in the breeze while the stars and moon shone brightly.

"Of all places," she muttered, "I had to land in a forest."

Having had enough of the nocturnal view, Alice decided to look for a place to stay the night. She didn't know this world at all and didn't want to stumble upon any dangers it might present. As she headed north, she kept her hand on her flintlock pistol. Alice knew the gun wasn't loaded, but she felt safer with a weapon in hand. It was all she had to defend herself. Even if she couldn't shoot it, it could still provide a painful blow to the head.

After walking for what felt like hours, Alice found an abandoned house. Half the roof had caved in, and vines climbed up the walls. The inside of the house was a mess, but she managed to find a corner where she could lie hidden in the dark. Although she was tired from walking. she wasn't comfortable enough to fall asleep.

Her thoughts traveled to Dorothy and where she might be. Alice decided to find her first thing in the morning. They couldn't have landed too far apart, and she was convinced there was a town nearby. Finally, as her thoughts calmed down, Alice unknowingly drifted off.

. . .

The next day, Alice was awoken not by the rising sun but by the growling in her stomach. She was hungry and didn't want to wait any longer to find something to fill her up.

Leaving the house, all Alice could think about was food. The warm rays of light slipping through the trees felt like it was no longer morning, which explained why her stomach had notified her of hunger. Placing her hand on the pistol in its holster, Alice continued north.

After a couple minutes, she noticed smoke rising above the trees. She picked up speed. It didn't seem to be coming from far away. Strangely, though, there were no signs of a town nearby—no sounds of people, and the trees weren't thinning out. Alice decided to play it safe and slowed down, cautiously making her way toward the smoke. Although she was the kind of girl who loved risks and wouldn't mind an adventure, she was smart enough to be alert when in unknown territory.

Nearing the source of the smoke, Alice was glad she hadn't made too much noise. The smoke was rising from a big black pot of stew bubbling over a fire. A humongous twenty-foot-tall troll was stirring the stew, his belly resting heavily on his legs. Another pale-green troll sat across from him, picking his teeth with a bone. They didn't look too scary; Alice was more disturbed by how ugly and dirty they were.

Staying out of sight behind a tree, Alice listened to their boring conversation.

"I don't know why Mama wants us to go home," the troll stirring the stew said. As he spoke, his saliva flew from his cracked lips and landed in the pot.

"It's safer back up north. The New Queen is not friendly," the other replied. His rotten teeth gave Alice the shivers. They were disgusting, and the more she watched them, the more she felt like gagging.

"We haven't said hi, how does Mama know she's not friendly?"

"Mama knows. Is the stew done yet?"

"Almost, I just need the rabbits."

Alice didn't see any rabbits hopping around, and neither of them made a move to catch any.

The foul-mouthed troll answered her unspoken question.

"What is taking Pigpen so long?"

Immediately, Alice crouched down. The sudden realization that there was another troll out of sight meant it was time to get going. But before she could sneak away, she felt someone pulling her by the leg and hanging her upside down.

"Look, brothers! I've found a human!" Pigpen exclaimed as he shuffled toward them with Alice swinging from side to side.

"Put me down!" she ordered, but none of them listened.

"You kidnapped her?" the troll by the pot asked in shock.

"No, no. I'm not stupid. I found her hiding behind the trees."

"What was she doing behind the trees?"

"I don't know," Pigpen said as he tossed a bag of rabbits to the ground.

"Put me down, you stinking beast!" Alice ordered once more, and this time she caught their attention.

Pigpen, who seemed to be the youngest, released his grip. Alice landed flat on her stomach, the air in her lungs forcefully escaping. Without waiting for the others to react, she tried to scramble to her feet. But before she could stand up, one of the trolls placed his heavy hand on her back, and air whooshed out of her again as he pinned her down.

"Are you stupid? We can make use of her," the troll with the rotting teeth said to his dimwit brother.

"Great, you're going to eat me!" Alice looked up and glared.

The troll and his brothers awkwardly chuckled. She only rolled her eyes in response as she tried to pull herself out from under the troll's hand.

"Eat you? We're not going to eat you, you humans taste very bad."

"Well, if you're not going to eat me, then let me go," Alice snapped.

"No, we're not going to eat you. We're going to take you home with us."

"What use am I there?" Alice attempted to reason.

"Your innards are very useful. Mama can use them for all kinds of things."

"My innards? I have horrible innards. I eat horrible things and they're useless," Alice replied.

"You're so pretty, with pretty hair and pretty skin. Your innards are only useless if you look like us," the troll said.

Alice gave up reasoning with them when they tied her up with thick rope and sat her near the bubbling pot. When they offered her the brown stew, she declined. All she could do was sit and watch, until she came up with an escape plan.

CHAPTER 14

Toto flapped his wings and glided high above the trees. The cool breeze made it a good day to fly around aimlessly, but he had a job to do. Dorothy had asked him to look for Alice. She was sure they hadn't landed too far away from each other. So, in the form of an eagle, Toto circled the area for a glimpse of her.

As he flew over a shallow river and trees, he heard a familiar voice. Heading in its direction, he found three ugly trolls and a girl tied up with ropes in the forest. The trolls were moving rather slowly as they attempted to travel undetected, but the girl was not as concerned about keeping their cover.

"How far is your home?" the girl asked.

"Not far," one of the trolls replied.

"At this pace, it's very far," she said.

It didn't take Toto long to realize that the girl was Alice. He didn't have to sniff her hand to know it was her or come any closer to recognize her snappy character.

Not wasting any more time, he flew back at full speed to the nearest town and swooped down toward the window of a tavern. There he found Dorothy sitting at a table near the window, reading the traveler's journal. Toto immediately flapped his wings, sending her their agreed signal.

Looking up from the journal, Dorothy whispered, "Did you find her?"

He flapped his wings again in reply. Dorothy nodded and gestured that she'd meet him outside. Toto returned to his original form and began leading Dorothy into the forest, stopping to look back at her every time he went too far ahead. She was doing her best to keep up, but she just wasn't as fast as he was.

"Is she very far?" Dorothy asked as she climbed over a fallen tree trunk.

Toto barked in reply.

"Not sure if that was a yes or a no, Toto," Dorothy replied. She was getting exhausted—they'd been walking briskly for quite a distance.

Toto barked again.

"Can we slow down?" she asked, and Toto dropped his pace by half.

"Thank you," she said.

They continued to walk for a few hours until they reached a wide, shallow river. The white pebbles of the riverbank and the smell of fresh water stopped Dorothy in her tracks.

"Let's stay here for the night," she said, looking up at the sky. It was already late evening, and the orange in the sky was slowly darkening. She didn't think it was wise to travel in the forest at night, nor did she have the energy to keep going.

Sitting on a big gray rock, she said, "Why don't you check to see how far away Alice is?"

Toto responded with a bark before magically transforming into a bird and taking flight. Dorothy watched as he gracefully spread his wings and disappeared into the sky. She wondered what it would be like if he were always a bird, but she loved him more as the little black dog.

Knowing Toto would take awhile, Dorothy lay back against the rock and shut her eyes. With one of her senses muted, the rest of them immediately sharpened. She realized something was off. Straining her ears, she listened for any sound that was out of place, and when she heard it, she bolted upright.

Dorothy set the journal down and hopped off the rock. She moved forward cautiously but abruptly stopped when she heard the sound again. This time the flapping of wings sounded close, as though it was right behind her. But before her instinct to turn around kicked in, a feathery hand swung across her chest and gripped her throat.

Dorothy felt herself being dragged backward as she struggled to free herself from the unknown attacker's grasp. But no matter how hard she tried, his grip was too strong. She was weakening. Gasping for air, Dorothy acted on the only idea that popped into her head and reached for her whip. Releasing it, she swung it backward. The loud snap was followed by a cry of pain.

Feeling the grip loosen around her neck, Dorothy pushed herself forward and inhaled deeply. She couldn't take too long to recover, though, and turned to face her attacker. When she saw who it was, she straightened up and drew her whip to her side.

The attacker, one of the New Queen's feathered guards, pulled out two short swords, ready to charge. Dorothy had no time to think through her next move and aimed her whip at his right hand. It looped around his wrist. She pulled hard, and the sword fell from his hand. Before he could go on the offense, Dorothy slashed the ground with her whip. It swiftly knocked one of the pebbles loose, which flew toward the attacker's face. He managed to block it with his arm, but he didn't anticipate the attack coming from the other side.

Toto dove toward the guard with his talons wide open and began to claw his face. The guard waved his hands and swung his remaining sword but he failed to free himself. When Dorothy saw the opportunity, she looped her whip around his sword and pulled it out of his hand. Now without a weapon to defend himself, the attacker quickly grabbed the traveler's journal and ran off.

He ran as fast as he could, not even turning around to check if he was being followed until he had put some distance between them. When he saw that neither Dorothy nor Toto had come after him, he changed into a giant raven and flew up into the night sky. His talons gripped the traveler's journal tightly as he made his return to Emerald City.

When he finally arrived at the palace, he headed straight to the New Queen's chamber. The windows were open, but he didn't enter until the New Queen acknowledged him. Returning to his original form, with blood dripping from his cheeks, he immediately knelt down on one knee. It wasn't customary to kneel in Wonderland, but he wanted to keep his head.

"So, is that wretched earthling dead?" the New Queen asked.

"No, Your Highness. She was not alone and—"

"How dare you return—"

"But I found something! Something that will surely interest you!" He risked interrupting her and offered her the traveler's journal.

The New Queen grabbed the book from him and threw it to the ground. She was about to order his execution when a familiar scrawl caught her eye.

Quickly picking up the book, she ordered, "Get out of here! The smell of your blood is giving me a headache. And don't come back unless you have her head!"

"Yes, Your Highness."

Alone with the book, the New Queen held her breath as she flipped through the pages. When she reached the page about Alice, she noticed something had been taken. The label under the missing sample read A PIECE OF ALICE'S DRESS.

She knew her worst enemy had arrived. It felt just like the good old days. This time, however, she was not going to let her go.

CHAPTER 15

Spending the night with trolls wasn't ideal. They weren't quiet sleepers, and their mouths didn't stay shut for more than a minute. As they drooled their way through the night, Alice attempted to free herself from the tree she was tied to.

If there was one thing she could give the trolls credit for, it would be their knot-tying skills. None of the knots were loose enough to wriggle out of, and moving her arms was almost impossible. Finally, Alice gave up and watched the trolls instead. She wondered where Dorothy was and if she was looking for her. Not wanting to count on anyone to save her, Alice tried to come up with another plan. When she finally gave up on that as well, she shut her eyes and tried to sleep, hoping a dream could spark a clever idea.

When morning came, Alice was awakened by a smell that made her gag. Pigpen was looking at her intently and chuckling at whatever his pea-sized brain thought was humorous. His horrid breath blew right into her face, which snapped her awake almost immediately. If it weren't for the ropes, she would have scrambled away.

"Oh, for crying out loud, don't come so close," Alice said.

"Why?" Pigpen asked. Alice held her breath.

"Your breath stinks, that's why," she snapped.

Pigpen merely shrugged in reply and walked off into the forest. He was probably going to catch more rabbits—she saw the other two trolls preparing breakfast. She watched them add strange-looking ingredients to the boiling pot.

"Aren't you going to feed me?" she asked.

"Thought you said you didn't want our stew?"

"I don't want it, but I have to eat," Alice pointed out.

"We'll feed you later."

"Why don't you just let me hunt my own food?" Alice asked, hoping their brains processed information even more slowly in the morning.

"Do you think we're stupid?" the oldest troll with the rotten teeth asked.

"You're stupid if you're going to let me starve! If I die, my innards are useless to your Mama," Alice replied.

The troll who seemed to always be on stirring duty looked at his brother with a look on his face that said, "She's right, you know."

"So, are you going to let me hunt or not?" Alice asked when neither troll responded.

They made strange faces at each other, communicating silently. When they finally came to a conclusion, the oldest troll got up and approached her.

"I'll go hunting with you," he said.

"Great. You'll probably scare the animals."

"We trolls can walk very quietly if we want to," he said with pride.

Just then, as though to prove him wrong, Pigpen came crashing through the trees. The earth trembled, and the trees shook so violently that they lost their leaves, as the troll's heavy feet landed one at a time. His footsteps were so loud, Alice held back her sarcastic remark, knowing he wouldn't hear it.

When Pigpen reached them, there was horror on his face.

"There's a beast!" he yelled. "It's coming after me! We have to go!"

His thundering shouts immediately made Alice's ears ring.

"Lower your voice," his brother hissed.

"It's coming! It will kill us all!" Pigpen whispered urgently.

"What beast? Where did you see it?"

"I saw . . . I saw it . . ." Pigpen paused as he looked where he came from.

"I don't see any beast," the troll by the pot said as he kept stirring.

Since the trolls had their backs turned to their brother manning the pot, Alice was the only one who saw what happened next. As he tasted the disgusting stew, two large claws shot out from the bush behind him and pulled him backward. Alice watched with wide eyes as the troll's head then flew from the bush and landed into the pot with a splash.

Turning around to see what had happened, the trolls saw the pot fall over, and their brother's head rolled in the spilled stew.

"It got him!" Pigpen shouted.

"Shut up!" his brother cried.

They stood back-to-back, darting their heads in the direction of any suspicious sounds, while Alice hoped the beast would not come after her next.

"What do we do now?" Pigpen whispered.

"We—we run," his brother replied.

As they began to clumsily edge away from her, Alice said, "Wait, you can't leave me tied up!"

The two of them looked at her simultaneously. The moment she caught their blank expressions, something flashed in front of Alice, and Pigpen slipped forward. His brother attempted to pull him back to his feet, but as he reached down to help him, something pulled his leg backward. The sudden tug sent him sprawling, the earth shaking when he hit the ground.

Alice had no idea what was going on. Something was moving extremely quickly and somehow stopped both trolls from getting to their feet. When Pigpen finally managed to stand up, the beast jumped right at him and dragged him away. Again, Alice did not see what happened clearly, and neither did the remaining troll.

"Pigpen!" the troll shouted. He didn't go after Pigpen, though. Instead, he began to crawl in the opposite direction. His heavy hands slammed down as his body crashed through the trees. He looked like a giant human baby.

Unfortunately, his efforts to escape were useless. He'd barely gone any distance when something pulled his right hand out from under him, causing him to crash face forward to the ground. Then, before he had a chance to react, his head was pulled back. Marks on his neck appeared. An invisible force seemed to be choking him, slowly digging into his skin. After a few useless attempts at grabbing his own neck, his eyes froze and he slumped down, dead.

Alice stared at the dead troll for what felt like a long time, uncertain what to do next. When she was finally ready to try freeing herself, she felt a quick gust of wind brush against her cheek, and at that very same moment, the ropes around her fell free.

When she got to her feet, she pressed her back against the tree in shock.

"I'm sorry if I scared you," Dorothy said, appearing in front of Alice.

Quickly recovering, Alice asked, "Was that you all along?"

"Yes. I'm really sorry for scaring you, though."

"Don't be. How did you do all that?"

"I have a little bag of tricks," Dorothy replied and tapped the sack hanging from her vest.

"Right, of course. So that beast was you too?" Alice asked, looking around.

"No, that was Toto."

At the sound of his name, the small dog ran out of a bush toward them. His tail wagged in excitement as he greeted Alice with a bark.

"Speak of the devil," Alice muttered. She had no idea how a tiny dog could change into a giant beast, but she was counting on Dorothy to fill her in.

"I'll explain later," Dorothy simply said.

Alice expected it would take hours.

CHAPTER 16

The three of them didn't wait for the dead trolls to start rotting before they began on their journey. They were far from the nearest town and had no time to waste. The long walk gave them more than enough time to talk.

As Toto took the lead, Alice asked, "Where are we going?"

"Scarecrow's place," Dorothy replied as she hooked her whip through the adjustable belt on the side of her vest.

"Scarecrow?"

"He's a friend. But the New Queen has him locked up in the dungeons."

"I see. What has the New Queen done so far?" Calling the Queen of Hearts *the New Queen* was rather strange for Alice, but the new name made her seem more docile.

"When I was in Emerald City, I heard people say she took all the magic and then banned it. Those caught practicing magic are to be immediately killed."

"Sounds like her. When I was in Wonderland, she was petitioning for the death sentence in place of banishment. I bet she's enjoying herself now."

"That's why we have to stop her," Dorothy said.

"And I'm all for it."

Dorothy told her what she needed to know about Oz, including Emerald City and all the different people in the land. She asked Alice about the creatures she'd seen with the New Queen. From her description, it didn't take Alice long to figure out what they were. Then it was Alice's turn to tell her story about her encounter with the New Queen—that is, the Queen of Hearts.

Alice was just a child when she first met the Queen of Hearts. She was painting flowers at the royal palace when the Queen of Hearts asked her a question she didn't know the answer to. The queen mistook her innocence for disobedience and banished her to the wastelands. Thankfully, the king talked her out of it and instead sent Alice away.

Alice then lived with the villagers in Wonderland. She had tea with Hatter and March Hare and learned about the people's suffering. She couldn't do much to help, but she befriended them and listened to their stories. When the Queen of Hearts found out that Alice was still alive, she sent her guards to kill her. Despite being hunted and almost losing her life multiple times, Alice returned to the palace and demanded an audience with the queen.

The court was visibly nervous when Alice questioned the Queen of Hearts's ability to rule. She accused her of being cruel and insane and proposed that a new queen take her place. When the people heard that a child was fighting for their rights, they began to speak out too—which started a war. But just as the traveler's journal related, the Queen of Hearts eventually won with her brutality and magic. Alice was forced to leave Wonderland for her own safety and has never returned.

"That's quite a story," Dorothy said.

"Well, that's not what my parents think."

"At least you know you're not crazy," Dorothy pointed out.

Alice replied with a chuckle as they finally reached a wide river. She didn't realize her story would take hours, but by the time she'd finished, the sun was ending its shift.

"We'll rest here tonight and continue on tomorrow," Dorothy said. Turning to Toto she said, "Can you catch us some fish?"

Toto barked in reply and ran to the river. He brought back dinner, and Dorothy started a fire. Alice helped her prepare the fish. She rarely cooked back home, but it was hard to forget the things she'd learned in Wonderland.

When they all finally settled down for the meal, Alice said, "So, after everything you've said, you still haven't told me one thing."

"What?"

Looking at Toto devouring a fish, Alice asked, "Is he really a dog?"

Dorothy laughed and replied, "He is. But with magic he can shape-shift into any animal."

"What he was this morning was definitely not an animal."

"Oh, that. It's his most advanced form. I don't ask him to turn into it unless he has to. It's not easy for me to control him when he's like that."

"I see you don't have a name for *that*. Training him must be hard, then."

"Oh no, not really. He's just a dog back home."

"You're not from Oz?" Alice asked. She hadn't realized Dorothy was from somewhere else, but when she recalled what Dorothy had told her and her uncertainty, it made sense.

"No. I'm from Earth too," Dorothy replied.

"Oh, well, I guess we have one thing in common," Alice said.

When they were done with their dinner, they found a safe spot among a few rocks and agreed on watcher duties. Alice offered to do the first shift, as she wanted to think through her next move, and Dorothy didn't protest. While on watch, she decided there was one thing she had to do before going face-to-face with the New Queen—she had to return to Wonderland.

· · ·

The next day, Alice woke up to the smell of cooking fish drifting on the morning breeze. They had a filling, fishy breakfast before continuing on with their journey. The second half of their walk was shorter, and before evening arrived they reached a town.

"We'll just grab some supplies before we head to Scarecrow's," Dorothy said.

The town was small and quiet, and it had the friendliest people Alice had ever met. Despite the New Queen, they seemed rather happy with their lives. She couldn't help wondering if they were adversely affected by her rule.

After Dorothy had done all the shopping, they headed for a narrow road that led to Scarecrow's tower. It didn't take them long to get there.

"Do you have a plan?" Alice asked as they began to climb the steps.

"A plan to defeat the New Queen? Not really. All I can think about is saving Glinda and Scarecrow. Glinda's always known what to do."

"Right, the witch," Alice said, not sure if she'd be any help without magic.

Halfway up the stairs, Dorothy ordered, "Toto, run ahead and check."

Toto dashed up the spiral staircase, and a few seconds later his bark echoed down the stairwell.

"What's wrong, Toto?" Dorothy shouted.

Toto didn't return—he continued barking as though signaling to them to hurry up. They ran up two steps at a time until they reached the top.

Alice didn't see what the fuss was about when they entered the messy room. But Toto wagged his tail furiously, and Dorothy's eyes were wide with awe.

"Did someone mess the place up?" Alice asked, taking a quick look around.

Dorothy didn't answer but instead said, "It's all right. She's with me."

Alice was about to respond when she saw what they did—dozens of fairies fluttering around the room appeared out of thin air. Some were seated on the bed and stacks of books, while others hovered high above her head.

"What are you all doing here?" Dorothy asked them.

"We're going to rescue Glinda, and we need your help," a fairy replied.

CHAPTER 17

"What's your plan?" Dorothy asked the fairy with big, bright-yellow wings. The fairy wore a crown on her head, so it was safe to assume she was their queen.

"The vines around Glinda's cage are too powerful for a single fairy to destroy. I need your help to get us to her," the Fairy Queen said.

"Why can't you just fly in?" Dorothy asked, raising an eyebrow.

"Because they can smell us," the Fairy Queen answered.

Alice, who was looking through Scarecrow's books, added, "The New Queen's guards can smell fairies. In Wonderland, fairies have to hide in the forest far away from them."

The fairies nodded in agreement.

"Well, honestly, I really don't know how I can help you. There seems to be no other way to enter the palace," Dorothy said with a sigh.

The Fairy Queen didn't look disappointed, though. After a few seconds of thought, her eyes lit up. But before she could say what she wanted to tell them, Alice beat her to it.

"Maybe there's another way," Alice said as she pulled a crumpled map out from under a stack of books. When she attempted to push the books aside, a few toppled over, and the fairies seated on them gave a soft cry. "Sorry," Alice apologized.

Spreading the map on the table, everyone came in closer for a look. It was a simple drawing of a maze with labeled exits. One read PALACE DUNGEONS.

"This looks like a map of the tunnels below the palace," Dorothy observed.

"It seems your friend Scarecrow went on a little adventure," Alice replied.

"I'm not too sure if this is a good idea. I've been down there, and it's confusing," Dorothy said.

"That's why we have a map. You said we need Glinda, so I say we go get her," Alice said.

Toto barked in agreement, and the fairies nodded. Dorothy didn't have much choice and gave in. She led them to the entrance to the tunnels. Alice couldn't understand why Dorothy was so cautious. She preferred to act more and think less, while Dorothy always had to pause to contemplate. Alice would probably never understand Dorothy, and vice versa.

When they reached the steps leading down to the tunnels, Dorothy hesitated once more before descending. Night had finally come to rest over Oz, and the darkness below felt uneasy. The air was cold, and the directionless breeze made Alice wonder if Dorothy's worries were justified.

Out of the moonlight's reach, all the fairies simultaneously fluttered their wings, and their bodies began to glow. They were like fireflies, but bigger, brighter, and much more colorful. Their glow took away some of the eeriness of the low-ceilinged maze.

"I'm not very good with maps," Dorothy admitted as she picked Toto up.

Alice waved over a few fairies to fly closer in so she could see the map and replied, "Don't worry. I'm pretty good at mazes."

The rescue team followed Alice's lead, turning corners and descending more steps. Almost an hour later they entered the round chamber. The water dripping from the ceiling plopped loudly into a puddle, and strangely a breeze was trapped in the room.

As Alice stepped forward, Dorothy said, "Be careful. The floor slants downward, and there's a puddle in the middle."

"It's just water," Alice replied.

"It's not just water," the Fairy Queen whispered.

Turning to look at the fairies, Alice noticed they flew close to the walls, away from the puddle in the center. Dorothy noticed it too and looked long into the darkness that swallowed the chamber.

"Let's just keep going," Alice quickly said.

After they left the chamber, Dorothy asked, "What's in the water?"

"Nothing's in it," the Fairy Queen replied.

"If there's nothing there, then what's the problem?" Alice asked.

"There were once two strangers who visited Oz," the Fairy Queen explained. "They said they were brothers in search of stories. The two of them always carried around leather-bound books and wrote down all the stories they could find. Once they had enough, they entered that puddle of water and never returned."

"So it's a portal?" Dorothy said, thinking aloud.

"Yes. But whoever enters that portal never returns. It is best to stay far, far away from it."

Dorothy nodded, but Alice was curious. The two strangers sounded familiar. Something told her she knew them, and she couldn't shake off the feeling.

"What were their names?" she asked.

The Fairy Queen thought for a while. She didn't seem to be able to recall their names, so the other fairies whispered possible answers to her. When she heard the right one, she confidently said, "Jacob and Wilhelm."

"The Brothers Grimm?" Dorothy quickly asked to confirm the name.

"Grimm, yes. Strange name for strange men," the Fairy Queen said.

"Do you know them?" Alice asked Dorothy.

"No, I don't. But I do know they are dead."

Alice narrowed her eyes. "They can't be. I've met them."

"I think you're mistaken," Dorothy said. "The Brothers Grimm have been gone for years. I've read their books."

"Then how would you explain the journal?" Alice challenged.

"The one about Wonderland? That's by them?" Dorothy failed to hide her shock.

Dorothy was having a hard time believing her, but Alice was sure she knew the brothers. They were the ones who'd told her about Cheshire Cat. She'd trusted them because they'd always listened to her stories. Alice had to admit that the brothers hadn't looked very young when she'd met them, but they hadn't looked sick or weak either. As much as Dorothy found it hard to believe they were alive, Alice found it hard to believe they were dead.

As the two of them puzzled over why they couldn't agree on the brothers' fates, their journey down the tunnels abruptly halted. Toto's bark snapped them out of their reverie, and they found themselves standing in front of a wall.

"Are we lost?" the Fairy Queen asked.

Alice took a long look at the map, then said, "No. We're here."

Handing the map to Dorothy, she pressed her ear to the wall and listened. Through the old bricks and cracked cement, Alice heard faint, muffled voices. "We're here. The dungeons are just behind this wall."

The Fairy Queen and her army fluttered down to the wall and gestured for the others to stand back. They blew red dust from their palms, which stuck to the bricks with a soft, pulsating glow. When the dust settled, the wall looked like the night sky full of stars. But there wasn't much time to admire it, as the wall began to crumble. It didn't fall with a loud crash but disintegrated into dust, leaving a line of powder where it'd once stood.

As the torch from the hallway shone brightly into the dark tunnel, Dorothy put Toto down and whispered, "Check if it's all clear."

Toto licked Dorothy's cheek in reply before he disappeared. Now all they had to do was wait. And hopefully in the meantime, no guard would wander their way.

CHAPTER 18

It wasn't long before Toto trotted back to them. His tail was wagging high in the air, and he barked softly.

Exiting the tunnel, they found themselves in a hallway that forked. When everyone trusted Toto and headed right, Alice said nothing and followed. The hallway led to another one that echoed with the voices of guards. Toto hopped as though to insist they were heading in the right direction.

Alice and Dorothy leaned against the wall and listened to the guards' strange conversation about trees. They guessed there were only two guards. Dorothy couldn't help wondering that nothing had been done to increase the dungeons' security. It showed on her face.

Hoping to stop any hesitation on Dorothy's part, Alice quickly whispered, "The two of us can take them out."

Dorothy exhaled and nodded as she armed herself with her whip. Alice took her unloaded flintlock pistol from its holster. Acknowledging Dorothy's unspoken question if she was ready, Alice walked out from behind the wall into plain sight. The guards were so caught up in their conversation that they didn't notice them. They spotted them only when the girls were a few feet away—and only after Alice cleared her throat.

"Who are you, and what—"one guard started to say.

"It's that girl! The earthling!" the other cried.

Alice didn't wait for Dorothy to react before she swung her pistol right at the guard near her. The barrel hit his head with a loud crack, and he stumbled sideways. Dorothy released her whip and snapped it around the other guard's neck. Jumping behind him, she tightened the whip until he went limp.

When the stumbling guard saw his friend slump to the ground, lifeless, he attempted to steady himself. Alice gave him a few seconds before she flipped the pistol, holding it by its barrel. Briefly weighing it in her hand, Alice gave him another blow to the head. The solid wooden handle did more damage this time, and the guard fell right next to his friend. Alice quickly reached for the keys at his waist as Dorothy whistled for Toto and the fairies.

Toto ran to them, the fairies trailing behind. Quickly, they turned down the walkway and ran to the end of the long line of empty cells. The fairies went straight to Glinda, who was unconscious. Alice watched the fairies while Dorothy unlocked Scarecrow's cell. They arranged themselves in a sphere around Glinda's cage and blew green dust from their palms. It rested on the thorns around the cage. Just when Alice was about to question whether the magic was working, the vines began to wither. In only a few seconds, the shriveled vines fell to the ground along with the floating cage.

Glinda began to regain consciousness, and Dorothy hurried to open her cell door. One kick shattered the cage to pieces.

"Glinda, can you walk?" she quickly asked.

"I'll help her," Scarecrow said as he hurried to her side. Although Glinda was awake, the vines had drained her dry.

Dorothy helped Scarecrow prop her up, while Toto and Alice ran ahead to check if the coast was clear. They heard footsteps in the walkway, and Alice waved for them to hurry.

"It's going to be hard to lose them," she said, ushering everyone into the hall. Once everyone had passed, she tailed them.

"We can create a temporary wall at the tunnel's entrance, but it won't hold for long," the Fairy Queen replied.

"That will work for now," Alice said.

When they reached the tunnel, the fairies blew invisible dust from their palms at the entrance. There was no immediate visible effect, and Alice held her breath when she heard the guards nearing. Everyone remained silent as two guards walked past.

Alice heaved an almost silent sigh when they didn't look their way. But just as Dorothy gave her a small smile, one of the guards retraced his steps and stopped right at the entrance. He turned to look at the invisible wall and tilted his head from side to side.

Alice quickly waved for the fairies and Dorothy to back away from the entrance and keep going. Everyone moved as more guards gathered at the entrance.

"They can smell us!" Alice hissed.

Moments later, one word softly echoed down the tunnel: "Fairies." All they could do then was run.

Scarecrow knew the tunnels better than any of them, so they didn't question his directions even when they didn't seem right. It was obvious that they were going a different way than they'd come, but no one took a second to ask where they were heading.

Finally, Scarecrow stopped in his tracks and pointed up. Although they didn't hear anyone behind them, nobody dared to make a sound. Alice noticed a ladder on the wall and didn't hesitate to climb it, pushing open a wooden door in the ceiling. She struggled to open it, and when she finally got it to flip open, a gust of fresh air brushed her face. An owl hooted, and crickets were chirping. They were in the forest. Once everyone had climbed out and was accounted for, Scarecrow shut the door and placed a heavy rock over it.

"We can't stay here. We have to keep moving," Scarecrow said as he helped Glinda.

Dorothy reached out to help him. "Where are we to go?" she asked.

"You can come with us. Our sanctuary will be safe," the Fairy Queen answered.

"Then let's not waste any time. The guards are not too far behind," Alice said.

"Follow me," the Fairy Queen replied and fluttered straight ahead.

Toto took the lead with the fairies, while Dorothy, Scarecrow, and Glinda followed behind with Alice tailing again. She wanted to swing her pistol at a guard's head if it came to that.

CHAPTER 19

The moon was full that night, hovering above the thick trees, but they didn't need its light, thanks to the fairies. Alice had to make sure she didn't fall too far behind the others. As they journeyed through the forest, she occasionally glanced over her shoulder to see if they were being followed. Every time she saw no one, she relaxed a little.

Alice didn't dislike all the guards—she knew not all of them were intentionally evil. Those who had followed the New Queen to Oz probably did so out of fear, so she found it hard to hate them. However, she also knew what they were capable of, and with the New Queen's magic, they were probably much stronger and sharper than they were before. Her looking over her shoulder every so often wasn't paranoia but caution.

After walking for a long time, everyone was visibly tired. Toto stopped bouncing around and kept his gaze straight ahead, while Scarecrow and Dorothy dragged their feet. The fairies were also flying more slowly, and a few even rested on Toto's back.

"I don't mean to sound impatient, but are we anywhere near your sanctuary?" Alice asked.

The Fairy Queen turned to look at her and said, "We're almost there."

"Why don't we take a break? I'm sure we're no longer being followed," Dorothy suggested and turned to Alice for confirmation.

"We're not being followed," Alice assured her.

Everyone slowed down, but before anyone stopped, Scarecrow said, "No. We should keep going. If we're almost there, we should keep going."

No one was in the mood to argue, so they continued. True enough, they were near the sanctuary, and it took them only another hour to reach it. By the time they came to a small lake with a delicate waterfall, all Alice could think about was soaking her feet in the cold water.

But she would have to wait. The Fairy Queen led them around the lake to the rocks by the waterfall. One by one, the fairies slipped through and disappeared behind the curtain of fresh water.

"You might get a little wet," the Fairy Queen said and gestured for them to enter.

Dorothy and Scarecrow carefully guided Glinda through the waterfall, then Alice followed with Toto. They found themselves in a narrow, dark cave. The fairies became a trail of light for the rest to follow, and with slow, careful steps they made their way deeper into the cave.

It was dark for a very long time, but the darkness soon faded when they reached the other side, which opened into a big area, tall like a column with curved walls. They stopped before an edge that dropped away like a cliff. Vines and flowers grew on the walls, in which the fairies had built their nest-like homes. The top of the space was open to the sky, and they could see the moonlight and water droplets gently dripping in, which would explain the puddle of water far below.

When the fairies saw that their queen had returned, they hurried from their homes to greet her. They cheered softly at the success of the rescue mission and stopped only when their queen quieted them with a wave of her hand. The Fairy Queen didn't have to give any orders, as the fairies knew what they had to do next.

They formed a line spiraling down. When all the fairies were in place, they blew on their palms and spread a pinkish, peach-colored dust, which clumped together to create steps that spiraled to the floor of the cavern. Even risk-taker Alice had to think twice about descending steps made of dust, but eventually they all reached the bottom of the staircase. From there, they entered an arched hallway lit with lanterns made of glitter. The hallway was large enough for humans. Wondering why, Alice was about to ask when Dorothy spoke up.

"Did you make this hallway for humans?" Dorothy asked.

"Yes, temporarily. We have guests staying with us, so we thought it'd be for the best," the Fairy Queen replied.

"Guests?"

"You'll meet them soon enough."

The hallway led to a large dome-shaped room with two flights of stairs that ascended to three levels. Each level had a row of arched doorways and a walkway that overlooked the giant tree growing in the middle of the room. Lanterns hung from the tree and the walkways' ceilings to light the dome. Alice looked around in awe.

When she finally pulled her attention away from her surroundings, she found Dorothy smiling at two figures that were hurrying toward them. One was a lion in green-and-black armor, and the other was a man whose skin was silver and shiny like metal.

"Brave Lion, Tin Woodman!" Dorothy called out.

"Dorothy! You're here!" Brave Lion replied in a deep voice.

Tin Woodman took Glinda by the shoulders and gestured for Scarecrow to follow him. Toto trotted after them while Dorothy gave Brave Lion a hug. She buried her face in his bright-orange fur, and he returned the hug with a gentle pat of his paw.

When Dorothy finally pulled away, she turned to Alice and introduced her to Brave Lion. "This is Alice. She's here to help us."

"It brings me great pleasure to make your acquaintance, Alice," Brave Lion said.

"It's nice to meet you too," Alice replied with a smile.

"Well, it's very late. Let me show you to your rooms, and we can talk more when the sun comes up."

When Brave Lion brought Alice to a tiny room, she threw herself onto the feather bed and immediately drifted off. She didn't even act on her last thought to blow out the lantern hanging from the ceiling.

• • •

The next day, when Alice woke up on her own without any trolls in her face or the smell of fish in the air, she felt fully rested. She sat up in bed and, wondering what time it was, hurried to the door. Pulling it open, she found Dorothy standing in the hall.

"Good afternoon," Dorothy greeted her.

"It's afternoon already?"

"Don't worry, I overslept too."

"Good," Alice replied with a chuckle.

"Brave Lion told me Glinda has regained her strength. Some of the fairies treated her overnight."

"That's great. Now we can ask her what our next move is."

"That's why I came," Dorothy said with a smile.

The two of them headed down to the tree where Glinda and a few others had gathered. Glinda was seated quietly in a chair while the rest had found a place on the floor and under the tree. When the small group saw them coming, they got to their feet and greeted them.

"Sorry we're late," Dorothy said.

"Not late at all, child," Tin Woodman replied as he gestured for them to take a seat on the tree stumps clustered there.

"We were just discussing what to do next," Scarecrow said.

Dorothy turned to Glinda and asked, "What is your plan?"

Glinda merely smiled and shifted her gaze from her to Alice. In a soft voice she said, "Alice, tell us your plan."

Alice was caught off guard. What did Glinda mean? With everyone's eyes on her, she thought over her words carefully. Then she simply said, "I have to go to Wonderland."

CHAPTER 20

"Wonderland?" Dorothy asked.

"Magic. The only way we can defeat the New Queen is to fight her on even ground. We need magic if we want to stand a chance," Alice answered confidently.

No one questioned her, and Glinda nodded in agreement.

"I'm going with you," Dorothy said.

Alice usually preferred to work alone, but she could use the company. She also worried that something could go wrong in Wonderland, even with the Queen of Hearts's absence. She nodded at her. Toto trotted up and barked. It was the kind of bark that meant he was coming as well, but Alice shook her head.

"I think Toto should stay," she told Dorothy.

Alice wasn't sure how magic worked between realms, because it was often unpredictable. Cheshire Cat once told her that magic taken from one realm to another became unstable and could diverge from its original purpose. If Toto went to Wonderland, he might unintentionally transform himself into the beast and wreak havoc. That was one risk she did not intend to take and hoped Dorothy wouldn't mind parting with her loyal dog. She was a little surprised when Dorothy did so readily.

Leaning forward to pet Toto, Dorothy said, "Sorry, boy. You have to stay and protect this place."

Toto dropped his head slightly with a downcast look in his eyes. But being the obedient dog he always was, he accepted the order with a soft bark.

"When do you plan to leave, and how long will you be gone?" Brave Lion asked.

"If possible, right away. We won't take long, two days at most," Alice replied.

"Go, and be safe. Wonderland might just be our only hope," Glinda said.

. . .

That afternoon, Alice and Dorothy stuffed themselves with fruit from the tree. The fruit was rainbow colored with a fuzzy, peach-like texture. Each bite was sweet, soft, and juicy and tasted like heaven. Neither of them had eaten anything like it before, and no fruit from Earth came close.

Once they were done with their lunch, they prepared a sack of black fairy dust with the dried rose petals Alice had brought with her. Their friends then stood around to see them off.

As Dorothy placed the sack on the floor, Scarecrow asked, "Alice, would you like a weapon to take with you?"

Alice shook her head. "My weapons are in Wonderland."

Scarecrow nodded and lit a match. He flicked it at the sack, and all eyes watched as the sack caught fire. After the flames died down, the earth beneath it sank, creating a dark, bottomless rabbit hole. The girls walked up to it.

Dorothy gestured for Alice to go first. "After you."

Alice turned to nod at Glinda before she stepped into the hole. Down and down it went, till she smelled mild, sweet cherry blossoms. Shortly after the familiar smell filled her nose, she landed on soft green grass. As she got to her feet, Dorothy fell right next to her, and Alice helped her up.

They were in the cherry fields of Wonderland. The blooming trees went on for miles. Alice remembered the last time she was there, when Hatter gave her a rose to bid her farewell. It had always been a sad place in her memory, but on this day, sad was far from what she was feeling.

"Wow, I've seen these trees before," Dorothy said.

"They look like the ones from home, but they're different. The color of their petals changes according to the mood of the person who touches them," Alice replied.

"Really?"

"Try it," she prompted.

Dorothy reached for a blossom on the branch above her and watched as the pink slowly changed to a mixture of yellow and orange. When she removed her finger, the petal gracefully returned to its original color.

"That's amazing," she said with a wide smile.

"There's more, but we'll save the sightseeing for our next trip," Alice replied and began to lead the way.

"So, where are we going?" Dorothy asked.

"We're going to see a friend. He can get the magic we need."

"Let me guess, is it Hatter?"

"Hatter is to Alice as Scarecrow is to Dorothy," she said, and Dorothy chuckled.

. . .

They didn't realize that someone more sinister had also thought of Hatter. Ever since she'd learned of Alice's arrival in Oz, the New Queen had been brewing a plot to assassinate her. She imagined seeing the world through Alice's eyes, which for her, scarily enough, wasn't hard to do.

Rubbing around black game piece from a Go board, the New Queen thought of the one individual who would bring Alice to her. Crushing the piece to dust in her hand, she summoned three of her best guards. The one she'd sent to hunt down Dorothy had not returned, so the New Queen had given up on him.

"I want the three of you to return to Wonderland," she said with smile.

The guards bowed and glanced quickly at one another.

The New Queen spotted their darting eyes, and her smile disappeared. "Find Hatter and watch him closely. When Alice shows up, make sure she doesn't live to see another day."

She pointed at them, and an angry burst of black tentacles shot out of her finger, hit them in the chest, and sent them stumbling backward. Just as they steadied themselves, their bodies began to transform into crows. They were much larger than ordinary ones, and their talons were sharper than double-edged swords. With bloodshot eyes, they cawed, determined to fulfill their queen's orders.

This time, the New Queen was certain Alice would be out of her hair for good. She was definitely not in the mood for any more disappointment.

CHAPTER 21

The cool breeze gently blew, and the cherry blossoms rustled softly. The mild fragrance lingering in the air was therapeutic, but the peacefulness was deceiving. Wonderland was no doubt the same as it was before: high mountains with snowy peaks; winding pebbled roads; giant, clear lakes; and towns and cities that felt warm and festive all year round. The only difference was the uneasiness in Alice's stomach.

If she hadn't returned to find a way to destroy the queen, Alice would have carelessly skipped about in search of her friends. Wonderland had improved after the Queen of Hearts had left. However, she couldn't help feeling unsettled. No matter how hard she tried to shake off the feeling of foreboding, it was deeply rooted in her. Telling herself that the Queen of Hearts didn't know she was in Wonderland helped her focus on the task at hand, but the consoling words didn't carry much weight.

As they walked down the narrow road that led from the cherry fields, Dorothy asked, "How far are we from Hatter?"

"Not far," Alice replied. She turned to her, and a question popped into her mind. "Where is Grimms' journal?"

Dorothy looked at her and said, disappointed, "One of the New Queen's guards took it from me."

"What? When?"

"When I was looking for you in the forest. He tried to kill me. I meant to tell you, but it slipped my mind in all the commotion."

Alice finally understood why she felt the way she did. "We better hurry. If the New Queen knows I'm back, she'll step up her game."

Falling silent, they picked up speed. Alice led Dorothy along the path that entered the forest. They had to hike for a while before they reached a waterfall. Emerging from the thick woods, they had descended a wooden staircase before Alice saw the glistening lake and the waterfall that gushed from the rocky mountain. In the center of the lake was a gazebo. A path of large rocks led to it from the pebbled beach. On the shore of the lake, not far from the gazebo, was a wooden house. Unlit lanterns hung from its roof, and the windows were wide open. Alice took only one quick glance at the house before heading for the rock path.

Before taking a step onto the first rock, Dorothy asked, "Is that Hatter?"

There was a man seated in the gazebo, playing a game of Go by himself. He wore a conical hat and a suit with light and dark oriental patterns. He didn't seem to have noticed them yet and continued with his game.

"Yes," Alice replied.

When they were just a few rocks away from the gazebo's wooden platform, Hatter stopped midway in his move and tilted his head slightly toward them. Though most of his face was visible, his hat hid his eyes in shadow.

"Hatter, it's me, Alice," she said. She wasn't sure if Hatter recognized her. When she'd left Wonderland, she was merely a child. Now that she was nearing the end of her teens, Alice was afraid he would act hostile toward them.

Hatter didn't reply as he placed the game piece back in its original position. When Dorothy shifted nervously behind her,

Alice said, "This is Dorothy. She's from Oz, which the Queen of Hearts conquered."

"Hello, Hatter," Dorothy greeted him uneasily.

"Aren't you going to invite us for tea?" Alice asked, still not daring to take another step forward.

"Tea. What tea?" Hatter asked.

"Green powdered worms with strawberry-painted rose petals," Alice answered with a smile. It was a flavor she'd made up as a child.

"Alice," Hatter said with a small smile. He got to his feet and gestured for them to enter the gazebo. When Dorothy nodded at him, he tipped his hat in response.

Alice took a seat across from him while Dorothy stood by her side. She knew Dorothy felt uncomfortable, because Hatter was so hard to read. She'd felt the same way when she'd first met him, but after she'd gotten to know him, she'd realized he wasn't as mysterious and intimidating as he seemed.

"How have you been, Hatter?" Alice asked.

"Wonderful. I always win the game," he said with a smile. His eyes still remained hidden as he lifted his head to speak. "No matter how hard I try to lose, I always win."

"Who are you playing with?" Dorothy asked nervously.

"Who? You, me, anybody. Want some tea?" Hatter didn't wait for a reply as he reached for a porcelain teapot and filled an extra teacup. Alice reached for it and handed it to Dorothy, hoping the pink tea would relax her.

"I missed you, Hatter. Aren't you going to ask how I've been?"

"I know you're fine. You look fine," he said as he picked up a black game piece. "I missed you too, so did March Hare. Tea becomes tasteless without you."

"Where is March Hare?" Alice asked.

"Oh, he must have gone below."

She looked under the table. A brown rabbit was happily lapping at some tea. When he noticed Alice, he hopped out from under the table and let her pick him up.

"How have you been, Haigha?" Alice asked as she adjusted his bow tie.

March Hare didn't respond, resting on Alice's lap. He watched Dorothy with curiosity in his eyes.

"How long are you staying?" Hatter asked.

"Not long. I wish we could stay longer, but the Queen of Hearts is causing problems, and I must stop her," Alice said. "I need your help, Hatter."

"How can I help you?"

"I need magic. Powerful magic."

"I don't have magic, Alice. Cheshire Cat does," he said.

"His magic isn't strong enough. I need magic from the White Queen, and only you can get it from her."

Hatter finally lifted his head up high enough for Alice to see his eyes, and she held his gaze. His pupils dilated in and out. It was one of the reasons why people found him strange.

After a few minutes of silence, Alice asked, "Will you help me, Hatter?"

Snapping out of a daze, he stood up and replied, "Yes. Wait for me here, and make sure March Hare doesn't hop into the water."

When Alice nodded in reply, he strode off. The sky was slowly turning a dark shade of purple as Hatter disappeared into the forest. She knew he wouldn't be back till morning. Getting to her feet, Alice turned to Dorothy, who was smiling and swirling the tea in her cup.

"Are you all right?" Alice asked.

Dorothy nodded and cheerfully asked, "So, we wait here?"

Alice was now certain the tea wasn't a normal brew. Taking Dorothy's teacup and placing March Hare in her arms, Alice answered, "No. We're going to get my weapons."

"Alrighty then! I'm right behind you!" Dorothy replied excitedly.

"Right. Let's hope that tea wears off soon enough."

CHAPTER 22

Alice and Dorothy went to Hatter's home to retrieve a lantern before they headed down a narrow path along the lake. The path followed the edge of the clear water and led to some stone steps between two rock faces. After a few cautious steps down, they found themselves on a wide, sandy walkway, made narrow where the rock faces curved in. As night fell and the moon appeared in the starry sky, the rock face began to sparkle.

"Wow," Dorothy whispered with a childish giggle.

Alice remembered being awestruck when she'd stumbled upon this place. She'd snuck away from Hatter and spent the night there. It wasn't the safest place in the world, but it was beautiful.

After a few minutes, Alice stopped and waved Dorothy over. Handing her the lantern, she knelt down and began to dig in the sand by the rock face. Dorothy didn't say a word as she watched—Alice was rather sure it was the effects of the tea wearing off. Once she'd dug about a foot deep, she found what she was looking for.

Dusting off the sand, she pulled out a wooden box and a short sword. Alice wrapped her hand tightly around the sword's handle and pulled it out of its red sheath, the moonlight glinting off the metal. She slipped it back into its home and slung it across her back.

"That is one dangerous-looking blade," Dorothy said.

"Glad you're back," Alice replied.

"What do you mean?"

Alice just laughed and shook her head. She reached for the wooden box and opened it in the light from the lantern. In it was a belt with compartments holding three small bottles filled with malachite-, gamboge-, and razzmatazz-colored liquids and a deck of cards. Before putting the belt on, Alice reached for the two cards in her pocket, which completed the deck. She then took the bottle of gamboge-colored liquid and squeezed a drop of it onto the deck. Although nothing visibly happened, Alice knew it had worked.

As Alice hung the belt around her waist, Dorothy asked, "What's in those bottles?"

"Potions. Cheshire Cat gave them to me. He said they would be useful."

"What do they do?"

"This one corrupts, this one enhances, and this one does whatever its user wishes," Alice said as she pointed from the bottle of malachite liquid to the gamboge to the razzmatazz.

"It does . . . whatever?"

"Sometimes good, sometimes bad, all based on your intentions. I've never used it before."

"I see. So what did that other potion do to enhance the cards?" Dorothy asked, setting March Hare down and pointing at the bottle Alice had used.

Alice slipped a card from the deck and handed it to her. Dorothy examined the card and shrugged when she found nothing unusual. She returned it to Alice, who threw it against the wall. The card stuck. Dorothy tugged the card off the wall and looked at Alice for an explanation, eyes wide. She opened her mouth to ask a question but held her tongue and instead handed the card back to Alice, who returned it to the deck. Dorothy silently lowered the lantern and rested her hand on her whip. Alice gave her a questioning look, and she responded by tapping her ear. Alice listened. It didn't take her long to hear the soft flapping of wings.

Alice picked up March Hare and placed him into the hole she'd dug. Knowing he was safe there, she reached for the handle of her sword. But before she could pull it from its sheath, something sharp struck her hand—two large crows dove at them, while a third shot out from behind her.

Dorothy whipped at the one flying low, while Alice threw cards at the crows above them, but they dodged it all swiftly. One went straight for Dorothy, while the other two readied their claws and aimed for Alice. Unable to arm herself, Alice attempted to wave away the two crows snapping their beaks at her face but tripped. As she fell back, she saw Dorothy pull one back with her whip. Seconds later, she wrapped the whip around the other's neck and flung it against the wall. The third was already lying on the ground.

"Are you all right?" Dorothy asked, hurrying over to Alice.

"I'm fine." Alice quickly got to her feet and pulled out her sword.

"I have a feeling they're here to take our lives," Dorothy said.

"I'm right there with you."

Just then the crows straightened their wings and transformed into the New Queen's guards. They pulled out their blades and charged without a moment of hesitation. Alice swung her sword at one guard and kicked the other in the chest. She didn't need to worry about Dorothy—she knew she could protect herself. Between ducking and avoiding the blades swung in her direction, Alice caught glimpses of Dorothy taking down her opponent. From the corner of her eye, she saw her snap her whip at a guard. She slashed him five more times across his neck, and he choked on his own blood. Alice meanwhile managed to draw some blood but did no permanent damage. She couldn't beat them both and was extremely glad when Dorothy stepped in to help.

Dorothy used her whip to pull a guard away from Alice, who saw the opportunity to corner her opponent. Her blade clashed against the guard's. She was determined to win the duel. She quickly struck the guard's wrist, and he dropped his blade. She then kicked him in the stomach and knocked his other hand, which sent his other blade flying to the ground. He now had his back against the rock face. Alice lifted her blade in the air and was about to bring it down when Dorothy called out, "Alice!"

Turning her head at the sound of her name, Alice saw that the other guard had an arm across Dorothy's chest and held a blade to her neck. She responded by resting her blade on the neck of the guard who was backed against the rock face.

"Let her go," she said.

"You first."

Alice slowly reached for a card in her belt, but the guard saw her move.

"I wouldn't do that if I were you," he said as he pressed the blade to Dorothy's throat.

Alice looked at the guard at the end of her sword and threatened, "Let her go or I'll kill him." She pushed her sword into his skin, and blood trickled from the cut.

"Go ahead. Kill him," the other guard dared. "He's nobody to me."

Alice was tempted to finish off the guard, but all she did was tighten her grip on her sword so hard her knuckles turned white. *How are we going to get out of this?* She had no idea.

CHAPTER 23

Alice's head whirled with useless ideas, her palms sweaty. She thought of her options and found herself in check, like the king on a chessboard. Just as she was trying to figure out how to buy more time, she heard a swishing sound. It was rather faint, but she could tell Dorothy heard it too. She turned her head toward the sound and saw a spinning hat bounce between the rock faces. As though it had calculated its trajectory, the hat hit the guard on the wrist and jumped forward. It was going fast enough to leave a deep cut, and the guard dropped his blade in pain. It clanged to the ground, and the swishing sound temporarily stopped.

When Alice heard it again, she shouted to Dorothy, "Duck!"

Dorothy immediately crouched and rolled forward. She didn't get up when the hat returned. It slashed the neck of the guard who'd been at the mercy of Alice's sword and cut the other guard's face clean across. As his friend slumped to the ground, dead, the other guard touched the cut on his face. When he saw the blood on his hand, he attempted to utter a cry but flopped to his death before the sound could reach his lips.

Helping Dorothy to her feet, Alice saw Hatter put on his hat and amble toward them. He stopped to pick up March Hare.

"What is it?" he asked the hare. "More tea? Let's go, then."

Hatter didn't wait for either of them as he turned on his heel and headed to the stone steps. Alice and Dorothy didn't say a word, hurrying after him as he whispered to March Hare.

Once they'd finally entered Hatter's home, Alice asked him, "Did you get the magic? Did you see the White Queen?" Alice worried if he'd actually gone to see the White Queen. Her palace wasn't close, and he'd reappeared rather suddenly. She was afraid that Hatter had failed.

"She was looking for me," Hatter replied. He then reached into his pocket and pulled out a tiny box, which he handed to Alice. "Her Majesty said to give this to you when you return to Wonderland."

Alice quickly took the small box and opened it. When she saw what it was, she smiled. A large pearl shone in the candlelight, and she knew exactly what to do with it.

"Thank you, Hatter," she said and put the box safely in her pocket.

He merely nodded and placed March Hare on a floor cushion by the low table. Alice gestured Dorothy over and noticed a cut on her knee.

"You're bleeding," Alice pointed out. Alice also had a cut, but on her arm, and it was taking a lot of effort to ignore.

Hatter retrieved a shallow basket from a wooden shelf and placed it on the table. Dorothy pointed at the green paste in the basket and asked, "What is that?"

"Hatter's special paste," Alice replied.

They both sat down across from him at the table, and Alice attended to Dorothy's cut. She placed a thick layer of paste on her knee, followed by a few purple leaves, then wrapped it with a piece of cloth. Once she was done with Dorothy's bandage, Alice cared for her own wound.

"I used to fall while climbing trees, and Hatter had to fix me up. His special paste always worked miracles, and I'm sure it still does," she said.

"It's already a miracle that I don't feel any pain," Dorothy replied.

"That's how good it is," Alice said with a laugh.

When she was done, she returned the basket to its place, reminiscing about her days spent with Hatter. When she came back to the table, a part of her wanted to stay.

"Tea?" Hatter asked as he placed two ceramic cups in front of them.

This tea smelled different than the one before and was bluish in color. Alice knew what it did and drank from her cup without hesitation. A few minutes later, the world blurred and dipped into blackness.

. . .

When morning arrived, Alice found herself lying on a mat. Dorothy was sound asleep a few feet away from her. She thought about waking her up but decided to have a talk with Hatter first.

Outside, the cheerful morning in Wonderland made last night's battle feel like a dream. The cool breeze tingled her skin, and the soothing sound of gushing water made her feel at peace. As she headed toward the shore, she saw Hatter at the gazebo in the middle of the lake. He was probably finishing the game that was interrupted yesterday but didn't seem to mind when Alice joined him.

"Can I play?" Alice asked.

"If you aren't afraid to lose," Hatter replied.

Alice sat across him and made a thoughtless move. Hatter tsk-tsked almost immediately and took much longer than she did before he made his move.

"I'll be leaving soon," she told him.

"You must be careful," he said.

"I will. I'm just wondering if you would . . ." Alice trailed off, uncertain if she should ask what was on her mind.

"If I would come with you?" Hatter asked, as though he had read her thoughts.

"Yes. Would you come with me? I could really use your help," she admitted.

Hatter didn't answer as he took a sip of tea. When he put the cup down, he moved his game piece. Alice patiently waited for his response.

When she made another reckless move, he said, "You'll be fine, Alice."

"I just want you with me," Alice confessed.

"You have to grow up," Hatter replied.

"I have. But some things don't change."

"And that is what I'm afraid of."

She found what he said strange. Was he afraid that Alice wouldn't grow up, or was he referring to something else? It didn't take her long to figure out.

"I'll make sure she doesn't do it again," Alice said.

"Are you going to chase the Queen of Hearts wherever she goes?"

"One quick step at a time," she replied.

"One quick step at a time," Hatter repeated.

After the game ended, with Hatter winning just as he'd predicted, Alice got to her feet and bid him farewell. He didn't respond, but when she stepped off the wooden platform, he said, "Cheshire Cat sends his regards."

"Tell him I said hello too," Alice replied.

"He also said your friend might find the razzmatazz potion useful."

"Useful how?"

"Cheshire Cat says strange things. Good-bye, Alice. We'll see each other again."

She nodded and slowly headed to Hatter's house, where Dorothy was already waiting.

"Did some catching up?" Dorothy asked.

"Sort of. Let's get back to Oz," Alice replied.

"Where shall we spark the tornado?"

"I'll show you."

CHAPTER 24

Alice and Dorothy followed a narrow path through the lush green forest. They were now far from Hatter's home, and it was almost noon. Like clockwork, their stomachs began to grumble.

"Where are we going, exactly?" Dorothy asked.

"To the Field of Flying Flowers. It's not too far from here," Alice replied.

A few minutes later, they reached a small town. The main street was lined by white-brick shops that traded in all sorts of things. Some sold fabric, others sold strange-looking animals, but most sold food. Savory smells of cooking wafted all around them and made their stomachs noisier than they were before.

"Why does everything smell so good?" Dorothy thought aloud.

Alice was wondering the same thing and stopped in her tracks. Dorothy turned to her.

"Maybe we could ask," Alice said.

"Would they give us something?"

"Maybe," she replied.

Alice jogged along the shops and stopped in front of a red double door. Three children were kneeling off to the side, playing with colorful marbles. When the young boy looked up, he asked, "Do you have a reservation?"

"An old one," Alice replied.

He nodded and tapped on his friends' shoulders. The children went to the double door and pushed with all their might. As it slowly opened, Alice saw a pebbled walkway that led to a wooden bridge across a small pond.

"I don't think we can afford this place," Dorothy whispered.

"No harm trying," she replied.

"What do you mean?" Dorothy asked. Alice left her wondering in silence.

Dorothy followed her. Alice confidently crossed the bridge and stepped into the large, high-ceilinged restaurant. A waitress came to greet them.

"I think I have a reservation under the name *Alice*," she told her.

The waitress looked down at her small but thick notebook and flipped through the pages. The writing was tiny, but the waitress seemed to be able to read through it at top speed. A few pages before she hit the end of the book, she stopped, smiled, and said, "Right this way."

Alice followed her, with Dorothy still cautiously trailing behind. The waitress led them to a wooden table by a window and handed them two scrolls. As they sat on the stools and unrolled the scrolls, Dorothy asked, "How old is your reservation?"

"Very old," Alice said with a smile. "I wasn't even sure if I had one."

A crowd of colorfully dressed and smiling people chattered, laughed, and devoured the food they were served. Observing them, Dorothy said, "The people here are very different from your people."

"Life seems pretty good with the Queen of Hearts gone," Alice replied.

The waitress soon returned, and Dorothy left the ordering to Alice. Alice knew very little of the menu, but she ordered whatever sounded good. When the food arrived, the two of them gulped down both the savory and sweet dishes without a second thought. The flavors lingered on their tongues even after they'd swallowed the rest of the pink meat-filled buns and the warm stew with bright-colored vegetables. The flower-flavored tarts filled with custard and the tea with a pinch of salt were also hard to forget. Occupied by the food, neither of them said a thing as they ate. It was only after Dorothy had filled her belly that a worried look crossed her face.

"How are we going to pay for this?" she whispered.

"It's paid for. The day I left Wonderland, White Rabbit said if I ever returned, he would treat me to a meal at the Crimson Scroll Restaurant. He said he'd placed a paid reservation in my name, and I could claim it anytime. It was a very strange thing for him to say, because *anytime* is practically taboo to him. I'm a little surprised he actually made the reservation."

Dorothy laughed with relief. Stuffed, they exited the restaurant and continued on their journey.

As they left town, Dorothy asked, "Wonderland wasn't always like this, right?"

"Honestly, no. When I was here, nobody wore bold colors or smiled at strangers. Everyone kept their heads down and whispered. Even though the Queen of Hearts didn't rule this region, everyone fell to their knees anytime she appeared. It's a good thing she's gone, though I'm sure no one expected she'd take over another realm and terrorize it too."

"She won't be terrorizing Oz for much longer. I might be too optimistic, but with the White Queen's magic, we'll defeat her," Dorothy said.

"Yes, we will. And I'll personally make sure she does no harm again," Alice replied.

"What—what do you mean?"

"If I have to put an end to her, I will," she answered.

Dorothy briefly stopped in her tracks, unsure how to react, but after a few seconds she must have decided to drop the topic altogether.

"So how much further is this Field of Flying Flowers?" she asked.

"We're here," Alice replied, ducking under a branch and running down a short slope.

Dorothy followed her. As they ran through the field, the flowers uprooted themselves and flew out of the way, their petals spinning rapidly as they floated into the sky.

When Alice finally stopped, Dorothy caught up with her. Taking a deep breath, she said, "I have to say, Wonderland is wonderful."

"I couldn't agree more," Alice replied with a smile.

After they had caught their breath, Dorothy set the sack down and lit it on fire. A few seconds later, a tornado appeared where the sack had been and sucked them up. The flowers flew out of the way, and the blur of colors was the last thing Alice saw of Wonderland.

Moments later, they landed outside the fairies' sanctuary. They hurried inside, where they were greeted by their friends from Oz. Alice handed the pearl to Glinda, who examined it closely. She then handed it back and said, "Would you do the honor?"

Alice nodded, and Tin Woodman gave her a large hammer. She placed the pearl on the ground, and everyone instinctively took a few steps back. Standing alone in the center of her circle of friends, she raised the hammer above her head and swung it down with all her strength. Smashed, the pearl sent out a shockwave. Everybody stumbled backward, and the earth shook slightly.

Immediately after the tremor died down, Brave Lion asked, "Did it work?"

Everybody turned to Glinda and saw her white wand materializing in her hand. She answered, "Yes. Magic is back."

"And it is returned to those who inherited it," Scarecrow added.

The small crowd erupted in cheers. Even though it was only a small step toward victory, the return of magic had at least leveled the playing field.

They were now at war with the New Queen—and it wasn't going to be child's play.

3
INCURSUSQUE

CHAPTER 25

The ground shook, and the candles were snuffed out. Murmurs filled the hall as the New Queen got to her feet and eyed her fearful citizens. None looked like they knew the cause of the tremor, but she asked anyway in an eerily calm voice.

"Tell me, what was that?"

The people shut their mouths and shook their heads vigorously. Their eyes wide in terror, their pulses raced at the prospect of their deaths.

"You don't know?" the New Queen asked again, but this time her voice hit a pitch that bounced sharply off the walls.

The air in the hall became so still and cold that it raised the hair on the napes of everyone's necks and made cold sweat trickle down their foreheads. No one made a gesture; everyone held their breath. Even though the New Queen recognized their honest ignorance, she found their predicament rather comforting. The sight of them quivering in fear was exhilarating, but despite wanting to bask in their fearful presence, she knew the little tremor was of greater importance.

"Out with all of you!" the New Queen snapped.

The people unfroze and rushed out of the great hall. When the last scampering person was out of sight, she ordered her guards to bring the countries' leaders. She had a feeling that they probably knew what had just happened.

・・・

That night as the New Queen lay in her soft, silky bed, she found it impossible to rest her soul. Her finger that wore the diamond ring strangely throbbed, but the fear of losing her magic stopped her from removing it. Finally, when the moon slipped away and the sun came up to take its place, the New Queen gave up trying to sleep. She'd probably caught a few minutes of rest, drifting between reality and the dream world, but it was insufficient and put her in a bad mood.

As she stormed into the great hall that morning, she found five of her guards waiting for her. There was no sign of the leaders, and her blood began to boil almost instantly.

"Where are they?" she yelled.

Her guards flinched, and one boldly answered, "We went to their countries but found no one there, ex—except for Quadling Country."

"Spit it out, or don't say anything at all!" the New Queen shouted. From his stammering, she knew he was keeping something from her.

"Ev—everyone has gone to Quadling Country, Your Highness. An—and we can't storm the gates, Your Highness. They have magic," the guard replied, unsure what to say.

"Magic? Didn't I ban magic? You should have killed them all!"

"Your Highness, their mmm—magic is too strong. They have combined their powers and created a shield that our swords can't penetrate."

"They don't have powers, you fool! I took them, remember?" The New Queen raised her fist to prove a point, and her guards flinched once again. "It looks like I'll have to do it myself then!" she said, her face reddening.

Twirling her finger, she materialized black smoke out of thin air. Within seconds the hall was filled with the smoke. Moments later, the smoke dispersed, and the New Queen and her guards stood in front of a red-and-gold gate. Upon the New Queen's arrival, the people behind the gate shouted for their leaders to step forward. The Quadling girl and the leader of the Gillikins appeared faster than the New Queen expected they would.

"I summoned you to my palace, and you had the audacity to ignore me!" the New Queen cried.

"We don't have to answer to you anymore," the Quadling girl replied.

The New Queen laughed hysterically and called her guards over to catch them. But none of her guards moved. When she realized they were disobeying her, she abruptly stopped laughing.

"They're afraid, Your Highness," the Gillikin said. "We have magic!"

"Magic is banned! You will die if you practice it!" the New Queen shouted.

"You'll have to get us first," he said boldly.

She didn't think twice as she stormed toward the gate. She raised her finger and pointed at the Gillikin. Jagged streaks of dark-purple electricity shot out, but they shot back the moment the spell touched the gate. The magic hit her right in the chest. It was a powerful spell and sent her flying. She landed hard on the dusty pavement, and her guards rushed to her side. The New Queen shoved them out of the way and got to her feet. For a split second she considered charging the gate again, but the part of her brain that was less mad stopped her.

Taking a deep breath, she chose her words carefully and threatened, "I will be back. And I will kill you all!"

Motioning with her finger, the black smoke materialized once more and carried the New Queen and her guards back to the great hall in Emerald City. Once she was on familiar ground, she stormed off without a word to her guards. A few of them dutifully followed her, but no one said anything. They had no idea what she was planning to do. The New Queen was insane, and her insanity was both a weakness and a strength.

Once the New Queen had managed to calm down, an ingenious idea popped into her head: she needed to find a book in the royal library. If the people of Oz had really regained their magic, they were now a threat. Alice and Dorothy were probably the source of the problem, and soon they would use magic to destroy her. The New Queen was not going to let that happen. She was certain she could find a solution in the library. It had been Ozma's second bedroom, and it'd remained unattended since the New Queen had taken over. She'd never been the reading type and considered books an eyesore. But today the books would save her.

From the spies she'd planted all around Emerald City, the New Queen had learned about the Wicked Witch of the West. Her blackened heart had skipped with joy when the people of Oz had said she was far more evil than the witch had been. Although it pained her that she needed an ally, she had no choice.

Her plan involved her guards searching for books that mentioned this Wicked Witch of the West while she had tea. Each time a guard brought her a book that seemed relevant, she flipped through it. After a stack of books and countless refills of her teapot, the New Queen finally found the book that gave her the answers she needed.

"The Wicked Witch of the West was defeated by a young girl named Dorothy," she read out loud. "When the witch's family heard of her defeat, they retreated to the mountains in the north. The Good Witch of the South placed a curse on them that if they wished to remain immortal, they had to refrain from practicing magic. Otherwise a spider would appear on their skin and slowly kill them."

She forcefully shut the book. "Interesting." A puff of dust shot up, and the New Queen tossed the book aside in annoyance. Getting to her feet, she said, "I'm done with this horrid room. It's time to head north."

CHAPTER 26

It took more than a twirl of a finger to take them to the mountains where the family of the Wicked Witch of the West resided—even the New Queen's magic had its limitations. The mountains in the north had a strange habit of changing position, which made it hard for her to pinpoint the family's exact location. All she could do was direct them to a nearby grassy valley.

From there, the New Queen and her escorts started their hike up the tallest mountain. It was not a typical trek through the woods, but a difficult journey along a narrow, spiraling path carved from the rock face. But since she was the queen, she didn't have to break a sweat. Comfortably seated in her sedan chair, which was carried by a few of her panting guards, she didn't have to look at the scary drop-off that befell those who slipped. The New Queen simply remained in her cushioned seat throughout the two-hour hike.

When the New Queen finally stepped onto the rocky ground, a cold wind greeted her. It wasn't the kind of breeze that tingled her skin, but rather the kind that warned of an impending storm. Despite the chills it sent down her spine, the New Queen kept an upright posture and an emotionless expression to fit in well with the mood of her surroundings. As she took a quick look around, she found herself in a wide, rocky clearing. Behind her was the trail leading down the mountain, and ahead was a winding path that slithered between gigantic gray rocks. A broken, rusted gate marked the entrance to the witches' village.

Without any hesitation, the New Queen took the lead and gracefully edged around the broken metal pieces. As she walked up the path, a few of her guards took flight and circled overhead. She was glad none of her elite guards had lost their lives during the hike, but as for those who had, she couldn't care less.

After walking for a few minutes, she noticed the path grew wider. When it finally became as wide as a small house, she stopped in her tracks. Three green-skinned witches and a troll blocked her path. The witches looked around Alice's and Dorothy's age, and their impassive yet pretty faces matched their cold stares.

"I'm here to see your leader," the New Queen said.

"What makes you think she'll see you?" one of the witches asked.

"I have an offer she cannot resist," she replied.

"There's nothing we need."

"Oh, yes, there is," the New Queen said, pointing at a spider on one of the witches' necks. It wasn't an actual critter, but a tattoo-like spider with legs that slowly grew under the skin. It wrapped around her throat and reached down her thin arms. Based on what the New Queen had read, the witch did too much magic.

"Are you nearing your last days?" the New Queen asked. "I can remove that curse from you."

"Prove it," the witch said.

The New Queen smiled and waved for the witch to come closer. She hesitated, but before the New Queen's patience ran out and her actions became forceful, she boldly walked up to her. With a smile still plastered on her face, the New Queen wrapped her hand around the witch's neck. Slowly tightening her grip, she could feel a surge of magic escaping from her fingertips.

The witch's eyes grew wide in horror, but the New Queen was feeling merciful at the moment. When the surge stopped, she removed her hand and waited. It didn't take long for the ink spider to retract its legs and shrink to half its size. The other witches watched intently, expecting it to disappear completely, but the New Queen burst their bubble.

"Did you actually think I would heal you completely?" she said.

Now that they had seen what she could do, their cold stares melted to show their deepest respect. They wasted no time in showing the way to their leader. The witches' village was a rather pathetic domain. At every corner was a hut made of straw, and the green-skinned witches who called the huts home were an eyesore. Though it was so easy to despise them, the New Queen forced herself to focus on her goal.

Skipping the sightseeing, she reached her destination faster than she'd expected. The three witches brought her straight to the largest hut in the village. When she entered, she found herself standing before an older witch with spider legs reaching up her face. The New Queen said nothing as the witches told their leader what she had done. They then left them alone.

"I know who you are," the witch said.

"And I don't know who you are. But let's skip the formalities, shall we?" the New Queen said.

"Very well. What is your offer?"

"I will cure you and your girls of your curse and give you a home in Emerald City. You will have power over the citizens and can freely do whatever you want with them."

The witch nodded with a small smile. "And what do we have to do for you in return?" she asked.

"I want an alliance. We shall work together to make Oz a world to our liking, destroying whoever stands in our way."

"Is that all?"

"Of course not. I also want you to make me stronger."

The witch raised an eyebrow and waited for the New Queen to continue.

"I am sure that out of all your potions and spells, there is one that would make my magic stronger."

"Why wouldn't I just kill you and steal your magic?" the witch asked.

The New Queen laughed. "No, my dear. That is stupidity. My magic is too powerful for you to even touch. But if you wish to decline my offer, I shall leave you to your miserable life."

She would have preferred to kill them all, but their suffering was far worse than death. Not waiting for her to respond, she turned on her heel. Just as she was about to leave the hut, the witch stopped her.

"Very well. We'll join you, and I'll enhance your powers."

"What a wonderful decision! Now, when can we do it?"

"You need to give me a day. I have to write a special spell and prepare a potion in the light of the full moon tomorrow. This cannot be rushed," the witch replied.

"I can wait," the New Queen replied with a smile, "but I will need a nice place to stay. Something fit for your new queen."

The witch winced at the thought of having to submit to her authority, but she gave in anyway. The New Queen was provided a clean hut filled with cushions, fruit, and wine. Her guards were fed, and she was treated like the royalty she was. The witches disliked the idea of having a queen, but they all bowed their heads when they saw her and met her demands immediately.

The following night, the New Queen lazed in her hut while she waited to be called by the witch. She could hear the preparations outside and couldn't wait for it to be over. When her guard finally informed her that the witches were ready, she quickly jumped to her feet. Her new powers were only a few steps away, and she was ready for them.

CHAPTER 27

It was hard to see the stars that night. The full moon was big and bright yellow on the foreboding canvas of the sky, a flat shade of black. Though it was a perfect sphere, it cast a swirling reflection in the bubbling cauldron. The magical effect made the moon look like an ingredient being mixed into the concoction.

The New Queen edged toward the large cauldron and was surprised to find that the pinkish-looking liquid was odorless. The lack of smell made her skeptical.

"It's too pleasant," she commented.

"Some things are," the witch replied as she walked up to her. A troll handed her a parchment. She unrolled it and asked to hold the New Queen's hand.

"You better not try anything stupid," the New Queen said.

The witch didn't reply as she held her hand and began to read the spell. It wasn't in a language the New Queen understood, so she had no idea what she was saying. As the words left the witch's lips, the diamond ring began to glow. As it did, the throbbing on the New Queen's finger returned and began to spread through her hand. Just when it began to bother her enough to question it, the witch plunged her hand into the boiling cauldron.

For a split second the New Queen expected searing pain to shoot up her arm, but instead she felt a soothing sensation. The aching in her hand slowly died down, but as it did, her hand felt heavier. When she attempted to pull it out, the witch stopped her.

"Not yet," she said.

"Then when?" the New Queen asked, annoyed. The feeling of heaviness was starting to worry her.

"When it stops swirling."

Looking at the pink liquid, the New Queen saw the reflection of the moon slowly fading away. The ripples got thinner and smaller, and after a few minutes, the reflection of the moon disappeared. Not waiting to be told, the New Queen pulled out her hand. It was completely crystallized.

All eyes on her widened at the marvelous sight, but her eyes narrowed. As though the crystals had spread from the ring and rooted into her flesh, her hand sparkled brightly in the moonlight. Though she silently admitted to loving the new look, she was a little disappointed. It didn't feel the way she thought it would. No feeling of strength rushed through her veins. Her hand no longer even felt heavy. Not wanting to let her disappointment grow, she decided to give her new powers a try.

"Who wants to be cured first?" she asked.

None of the witches answered, not even the oldest witch. She merely smiled as she tossed the parchment with the spell into the fire under the cauldron.

"Don't you want to be cured?" the New Queen asked her. She managed to hide her annoyance.

"You should pick who you wish to cure, Your Highness. You're the queen," the witch said with a bow.

Those clever words were like giving a child a bag of candy, and the New Queen immediately placed her hand on the witch's shoulder. The moment her hand made contact with her green skin, she could feel energy flow from her fingertips. Her new strength was very evident. Silvery streaks appeared under the witch's skin and made the spider shrivel up and disappear.

When the witch was completely free of the curse, she and all the other witches bowed. Although the New Queen couldn't feel the magic in her blood, it was clear she had it. She was so obsessed with showing it off, she actually kept her promise. It didn't take long to cure them all of their curse, and when all the green-skins were healthy, the New Queen told them to pack up and get ready to leave.

. . .

The following morning, the New Queen tested her magic once more and twirled her crystal hand in the air. In a single motion, black smoke materialized and whisked them to the market in Emerald City in the blink of an eye. Their landing was almost perfect, and the people's screams were like music to her ears. The witches took flight on their thin black umbrellas and began to hex the terrified citizens right and left. The New Queen briefly watched them indulge their ability to do magic again, then retreated to her palace with the oldest witch.

Right in the very hall where the witches had once been banished, the New Queen kept her end of the bargain and made the witches citizens of Emerald City. She revoked the rights of the original citizens and gave them away to their enemies. She forbade the townspeople from leaving the city and forced them to live under the witches' rule. It was cruel, but the people were leverage. To top it all off like a cherry on an ice-cream sundae, the New Queen threw a feast to welcome her new friends.

The feast that night was lively and chaotic. The New Queen told herself to be less strict with the green-skins than with her guards, even though she wasn't very fond of them. She knew she couldn't afford to lose an ally and played the kind hostess to them the best she could. Once Oz was completely hers, she could do what she liked.

When the feast was over and drunken witches were sprawled out all over the messy courtyard, the New Queen retreated to her chamber for some silence. She briefly lingered in front of the mirror to flaunt her magic before Ozma and smiled when Ozma mouthed what were probably some ghastly choice words. Really, it was fortunate that the young dethroned queen was shut inside the mirror, as it spared her painful torture for being rude.

As the New Queen turned away from the screaming girl, she came up with a plan. Torturing Alice and Dorothy would be more fun than killing them. Her power shouldn't go to waste; killing the two girls would be a poor use of its true potential. She considered the plan a calculated risk. Convinced it was good, she summoned her guards.

"You won't fail me this time," she said and heightened their abilities with her magic. "Find where the girls are hiding. I want to give them a surprise."

After the guards took flight, the New Queen started to prepare for the next day. When morning came, she was going to go to Quadling Country and wipe that land clean. Not a single person would be left breathing—especially not after their rebellion. The thought of revenge was so sweet that the New Queen was too excited to fall asleep, as restless as a child on Christmas Eve.

CHAPTER 28

The gate stood tall and mighty. The New Queen's urge to destroy it grew along with a fireball in her crystal hand. When she couldn't hold it any longer, she threw the fireball at the gate. The moment the tongues of fire licked the metal, the flames spread and devoured the gate, leaving only a pile of ashes within seconds.

Confident her magic had prevailed, she stormed into Quadling Country and wrecked everything in her way. She was so caught up with destroying the houses that at first she didn't notice what was missing. It was only until she stumbled upon a doll that she paused to take a good look around.

"Where are the people?" the New Queen demanded.

Her guards shook their heads and immediately split up to hunt them down. She didn't wait for them and went on her own search. Unlike her guards, when she found no one, she stormed the houses and blasted their roofs off, angrily shouting and screaming, her urge to kill her enemies unmet.

When her guards finally returned, they brought not a single person with them. Quadling Country was deserted, and her possible victims had fled. In a last burst of rage, the New Queen ignited a tornado to destroy the entire country. If she couldn't destroy its people, she might as well destroy everything else.

Back in the great hall, the New Queen sat on her throne with an unapproachable look on her face. Even when her guards returned with good news, they stood outside the hall, trying to foist the role of messenger on one another. When they finally decided to do it together, they stood before their silent queen, unsure when to speak. The air was tense with silence. Finally, when the New Queen waved for them to start, their voices were rough and dry.

"Your Highness, we have found Alice," one guard said.

The New Queen slowly looked him in the eye, and he continued, "We sensed her presence among the fairies in the eastern forest. We tried to enter their sanctuary, but it's protected by their magic."

"It's a good thing you didn't enter," the New Queen replied.

Her guards looked at her questioningly, but she didn't say anything else. She took some time to think the good news through before she got to her feet and ordered, "Send for the oldest witch. Tell her I need a sleeping potion."

When her guards took off, she headed straight for the dungeons. Since the arrival of the witches, the dungeons had become quite useful. Citizens who attempted to escape occupied the empty cells, and it was no longer as silent as it had once been. Though the hallways now carried their ghostly pleas, there were still areas that were completely unoccupied. The New Queen headed straight to one of those. However, being down there reminded her of Glinda's, Scarecrow's, and Dorothy's escape, and she fumed to herself. It took a lot of self-control, but somehow she managed to refrain from destroying the dungeons with her magic.

A few twists and turns later, the New Queen stood in front of a special cell. The guards opened the door for her, and she retrieved a small black box. She brought it back to the great hall, where the oldest witch was waiting for her, her cauldron in the middle of the room. She was stirring a dark-green potion with a stick. It looked like any other potion, except for the lack of rising steam.

"Is this what I asked for?" the New Queen asked.

"Yes, Your Highness, a very powerful one too. A small dose can make a troll sleep for days," the witch said.

"Good. Bottle me a dose strong enough to make hundreds fall asleep."

As the witch filled up a small bottle, she said, "To make hundreds fall asleep, you will have to make each of them consume a drop."

"I won't have to," the New Queen replied as she took the bottle from her. Once in her hand, the green liquid inside the glass bottle began to evaporate. Soon, she was holding a bottle filled with dark-green smoke. The witch couldn't hide her expression of awe. Seeing her finally lose the pride she'd once had, the New Queen decided not to dismiss her as she had initially planned. Instead, she retreated to her throne and placed the bottle on the armrest.

With the black box on her lap, the New Queen waved her crystal hand over it and heard the lid pop open. She removed it and reached into the small box to pull out something small and fragile. The delicate-looking creature was a lifeless fairy. As she wrapped her hand around the fairy, streaks of black seeped into the fairy's pale skin. When the streaks stopped, the fairy's eyes shot open. Her eyes were briefly black before they returned to their original color. The New Queen opened her palms to let the fairy go.

It took the fairy awhile to fly, but when she finally did, she hovered before the New Queen. The queen created a small bag out of smoke, placed the sleeping potion in it, and gave it to the fairy. She didn't have to say anything—the fairy knew what to do.

"Fairies cannot be trusted," the oldest witch cautioned.

"This one can," both the New Queen and the fairy replied simultaneously.

"Look at that! She has no respect for you," the witch added.

"I am grateful for your concern, but I have it under control," both the New Queen and the fairy said at once. This time the witch understood.

The New Queen didn't wait any longer to send the fairy on her way. She fluttered out of the palace with the potion at her side and used her instincts to return home. Ravens trailed far behind her, ready to take position when she succeeded in her task.

After a few hours of flying, the fairy finally reached the little waterfall. Immune to the fairy magic that protected the place, she slipped right through and made it inside. When she entered the sanctuary, a group of familiar-looking fairies came to greet her. She had seen them before, but she didn't know who they were.

"Where have you been?" one fairy asked, her face filled with worry.

"We thought you were gone for good," another added.

She merely replied, "I'm fine. I need to see Glinda. It is urgent." She had no idea where those words came from, but they slipped so easily out of her mouth.

The fairies nodded and led her to the bottom of the cavern and down a hallway. When she entered the domed room, she saw two girls. They too looked very familiar. She felt like she had met one before, while the other looked like a memory.

"Tiny Fairy!" the girl with the blonde hair called out. "Where have you been? I thought you were . . . Never mind. What happened?"

She smiled at the girl before fluttering over to a tree stump. Once she'd planted both her feet on it, she reached into her bag and pulled out the bottle.

"What is that?" the girl asked.

She didn't reply—she wanted to but couldn't. All she did was raise the bottle above her head and send it shattering to the floor.

CHAPTER 29

The small bottle shattered like a fragile piece of porcelain, and the dark-green smoke began to spread almost immediately. Nothing could stop it from sending everyone into a deep slumber—nothing except for the little bubble that magically appeared around the fairy, which pulled the smoke into it like a vacuum. Almost immediately, the tiny fairy fell limp. The smoke remained in the bubble until Glinda strode over and flicked her wand at it. Everyone was still trying to process what was going on and said nothing even as the smoke turned colorless. Once there wasn't a single trace of smoke left, Glinda popped the bubble and picked the tiny fairy up.

"What just happened?" Alice asked.

"That was the New Queen's doing," Glinda replied, and the fairies gasped in horror.

"This means she knows where we are. It's not safe here anymore," Dorothy said.

"That's not the only bad news," a familiar voice said. Scarecrow had joined the crowd that grew since the tiny fairy's reappearance.

"What do you mean?" Dorothy asked.

"The New Queen has made an alliance with the Witches of the West. They have taken over Emerald City," Scarecrow replied.

"What about the people?"

"Those who tried to run were sent to the dungeons, and the others are barely surviving."

"Great," Dorothy said. She folded her arms, lost in thought.

Nobody shared anything with the group for a while, though whispers traveled through the crowd. It was heavy news to digest. Alice knew nothing about the witches but assumed they weren't harmless. Knowing the New Queen well enough, she had a feeling that the queen's making an alliance could only mean one thing.

"She's preparing to end this war," Alice stated, halting the whispers immediately.

There were a few seconds of silence after she spoke. Brave Lion broke them, confidently replying, "So are we."

All eyes were now on him, which he took as an invitation to continue.

"The Emerald City soldiers that escaped when the New Queen first arrived have made camp in a valley not too far from here, and I've just received news that the countries have joined them."

"That is where we should go," the Fairy Queen finally spoke, making her presence known. She then fluttered over to Glinda and gestured at the tiny fairy in her hand. "Can she be saved?"

"Yes, I'll attend to her right away. But while I'm doing that, you must make arrangements to leave," Glinda replied.

"I'll handle it," the Fairy Queen said. She turned to the crowd. "Be ready to leave when I return."

Everyone scattered. Dorothy went to help where needed, while Alice waited under the giant tree. There was little she could do, and she did not need to pack anything. As she watched everyone scurrying around, she thought about the war they were preparing for. Once night finally fell and the Fairy Queen returned to the dome, Alice had made up her mind on one thing. She wouldn't bring it up then, but she would have to soon enough.

Everyone quickly gathered around the Fairy Queen. Though there weren't many people who'd sought refuge in the fairies' sanctuary, it would still take them a while to leave undetected. There was no doubt the New Queen had her spies watching the place. They would have to slip under her nose to make their escape.

"The crows are watching the waterfall, and one fairy wing outside would set them off. The only way for us to leave is above." The Fairy Queen didn't have to explain further as she gestured to the open sky in the cavern. The fairies hovered in a spiral, each facing the wall. They blew fairy dust, and flowery steps materialized.

"After we make it up there, Brave Lion will take the lead. The crows seem to have sharper hearing as well, so please be as quiet as possible."

Everyone heeded her words and began to climb the stairs. The cavern was very tall, but no one stopped to take a break. Once at the top, the chilly night breeze blew on their skin. They were atop a large hill where thin trails of water flowed through the gaps between rocks.

Once everyone was out, including the fairies, Brave Lion went ahead. The fairies lit up to help him find the least dangerous path down the hill, resting on various rocks to light the way as he found his footing, which everyone else followed. By the time they'd descended, the sun was beginning to rise, and they picked up their pace.

Brave Lion assured everyone that they would be able to reach the camp before nightfall, but his definition of a fast-paced walk was based on his having four legs instead of two. As much as he tried to keep his promise, no one could keep up with him, and they were forced to camp for the night in the forest. But it was impossible for anyone to sleep that night. The fear of being caught rose at every unidentified sound. Even with people taking different shifts, no one had an hour of rest without peeking every once in a while.

When morning finally arrived, they were ready to continue. They'd covered most of the route the day before and reached the valley by noon. It was well concealed, its entrance blocked by large bushes. Brave Lion had no problem squeezing through the bushes, but everyone else struggled. When they finally made it through, everyone's jaw dropped. The valley was filled with green-and-gold tents, their flags flapping in the light breeze. Soldiers patrolled the area, and groups of people moved about. It looked like a festival, even though everyone was well aware that a celebration was not in order.

After the royal guards greeted them, they led them down the long line of tents. Alice and Dorothy saw troops at every corner, training and making weapons. Their sightseeing was abruptly halted when the two girls and Brave Lion were ushered into the biggest tent.

A huge map of Oz was spread out on a large table, with little wooden soldiers grouped around Emerald City. Standing by the table was a well-built man who towered over the other soldiers in the tent. When he saw them enter, he gave them a courteous smile and bowed low to Brave Lion.

"We've laid out the initial battle plan. Once we have your approval we can prepare for battle," the man said to him.

Brave Lion walked around the table and replied, "Explain, Captain."

The captain nodded. The other soldiers in the tent, along with Dorothy, Alice, and the rest of their group, edged toward the table. He cleared his throat, ready to begin.

"Before you start, I need to ask a favor," Alice said.

When Brave Lion nodded, she continued, "I want to face the New Queen alone."

"We'll face the New Queen together," Dorothy immediately replied.

"You won't see her during the battle. Despite her magic, she's a coward. She'll probably be heavily guarded while the witches fight for her. To defeat her, I must sneak into the palace and find her hideout."

"But you said she would be heavily guarded. How are you going to get past whatever is protecting her?" Dorothy asked.

"She will let me pass."

"It's too dangerous. She has magic; you don't," Brave Lion pointed out.

"Trust me. I'm going to take her down even if I have to go down with her."

Nobody said anything, and Alice took their silence as consent.

CHAPTER 30

Alice sat in her tent, staring at the three bottles of potion in front of her. She tried to think of a plan to defeat the New Queen, but her mind was blank. When she finally gave up, she took her flintlock pistol from its holster and set it on the table. If she failed to defeat the New Queen with magic, she would have to use the only weapon she had from Earth. Just as she prepared to load her pistol, Dorothy entered with Toto.

Dorothy saw the pistol and asked, "Are you going to use that?"

"If I have to," Alice replied.

Dorothy nodded before taking a seat. "Do you mind if I join you?"

Alice shrugged, and she smiled. She emptied her bag of candy and cookies on the table.

"What are you doing?" Alice asked.

"I want to sort out what's useful. That's the plan for now. What is yours?"

"I don't really have one," Alice answered honestly.

"What do you mean? Do you have a plan for when you face the New Queen?"

"Not really."

Dorothy fell silent as Alice fiddled with a potion bottle. Though the two had only spent a few days together, they'd been through enough to intuit each other's thoughts. They might not have become friends if they'd met on Earth, but their childhood worlds bonded them in a strange way. Dorothy held her tongue because she knew Alice would speak when she was ready, and she was right.

"All my life I've been told how to live. My parents arrange everything, and as their daughter, I do as I'm told. I grew up accepting their plans for my life until I realized I could control my own future. The day I fell into Wonderland, I was given a chance to make my own decisions, and the freedom to choose made me feel alive. But the freedom ended the moment I returned home. That's why I'm a bit impulsive when I get the opportunity to make my own decisions," Alice said, as though talking to herself.

"But are you willing to lose your life in the process?" Dorothy asked softly.

"At least I get to choose how I die. It may seem foolish to face my enemy without a plan, but it's a move I'm willing to make. I'm tired of living a small life, aren't you?"

Dorothy had to admit to herself that she felt the same way. She was living a small life back home, without any plans or a future. Her life was the opposite of Alice's, yet it also felt small. She wondered what she would do once she returned home. Would she go back to being a farm girl for the rest of her life? That glimpse of her future was troubling.

"I am. Our lives might be different, but at least we have one thing in common. I don't want to live a small life and need to seize the moment at every opportunity I get," she replied.

"So you understand."

"Yes, and I want to help you. I will bring you to the New Queen and wait for you to return. There's no *sneaking in* when we choose to live a big life. Besides, having me as backup is a better plan than having no plan," Dorothy said with a smile.

"Wouldn't that put you at risk too? That'd be stupid and very unlike you," Alice pointed out.

"No, it's a calculated risk. Toto will be in his beast form, and we can storm in to save you if things go badly."

"You can't even control Toto when he's a beast," Alice said.

"Calculated risk," Dorothy repeated.

Alice laughed, and the mood lightened a little. Even though she was still unsure about how to defeat the New Queen, she felt as though she could leave worrying for another day. When she was finally able to clear the dark clouds in her head, an idea fell into her lap. She uncapped the malachite potion and squeezed a drop onto a small lead ball for her pistol. The potion seeped into the ball, briefly making it glow dark green.

"Doesn't that potion corrupt?" Dorothy asked.

"Yes. Hopefully it does what it's supposed to do," Alice replied and loaded her pistol with the lead ball. Pouring gunpowder into the flash pan, she added, "I only have one shot."

Not giving much thought to her next move, she retrieved all her weapons and laced them with the malachite potion. From her short sword to every single card in the deck, Alice trusted the glow that illuminated them. When she was done, she turned to Dorothy, who'd been watching her the whole time. She still hadn't separated out any of her treats.

Alice asked, "Need help?"

Dorothy smiled, shook her head, and began to separate the ones she found useful from the ones that weren't. Alice read the labels on the wrappers, attempting to decipher what each one did. She paused on one large brown cookie labeled LINK.

"What does *link* do?" Alice asked as she picked it up.

"It temporarily links me and Toto," Dorothy replied.

An idea took root. Unwrapping the cookie, Alice set it down on the table and picked up the razzmatazz potion.

"What are you doing?" Dorothy asked with a raised eyebrow.

"I'm going to give this potion a shot," Alice replied.

"A shot at what?"

"At helping you," Alice said and poured the potion onto the cookie. But unlike what she'd done with her weapons, she didn't use just one drop. Instead, she emptied the bottle.

"Isn't that too much?" Dorothy asked, trying to hide the horror in her voice.

"Don't worry, this doesn't corrupt."

"But you poured the whole bottle! It might have some crazy effect. On top of that, the cookie is soggy now."

Alice shrugged as the cookie began to glow. Its glow was far brighter than they had expected, briefly blinding them. When it finally died down, she said, "Take a bite."

"You've got to be kidding me," Dorothy replied.

"Trust me. This is a calculated risk."

Dorothy hesitated for a moment but reached for the cookie and broke it in half. She then placed one half in front of Toto, who chomped it down happily, before she took a bite from the other. The crunching sound as they chewed proved how unlike a normal liquid the potion was. After Dorothy finished her piece, Toto jumped onto the table to lick up the crumbs.

"So, how do you feel?" Alice asked.

"I feel the same," Dorothy replied.

"I guess you'll only find out if it worked when you enter the battlefield."

"What if it doesn't work?"

"You have to have a little faith in magic," Alice answered.

"Is that your plan?" Dorothy asked jokingly.

Without hesitation, Alice replied, "Yes."

It might seem like a joke to Dorothy, but Alice realized it was the answer she'd been looking for. She had no clear plan to defeat the New Queen, but with a little faith in magic she might just succeed.

CHAPTER 31

The following week was both the longest and the shortest in the history of Oz. Time moved so slowly, but before one could question how, the sun set and the moon took its post. All the clanging and shouting rose to dangerous decibels, yet it magically didn't blow their cover.

Dorothy found the noise a little out of her comfort zone, so she retreated to a tent where the Winkies were inventing weapons. She was intrigued by their imagination and skill and volunteered to be their test subject. They were incredibly fast, and by the end of the first day, a prototype of a fireball thrower was ready.

The fireball thrower was a mechanical device attached to a glove. The glove was coated with a liquid that the Winkies refused to name but was supposedly able to hold a fireball. The mechanical device had a small gas tank and a trigger that sparked. To create a flame, the operator simply had to clench and unclench a fist, which pulled back and released a mechanism. The flame would magically collect above the glove, and the operator could then throw it.

Dorothy only roughly understood the concept, because the Winkies were so secretive of their trade. If it hadn't been for Tin Woodman, they wouldn't have let her watch them at all. When they'd murmured about a test subject, Dorothy had jumped to her feet and shot her hand high in the air. They'd hesitated until Tin Woodman had told them he thought it was a great idea.

As Dorothy pulled the prototype on, she felt a thrill shoot through her veins.

"Stand over here, please," a Winkie said and led her to a corner of the tent.

From there she was told to take aim at a piece of metal ten feet away. Without hesitation, Dorothy clenched her fist and silently squealed when a swirling fireball appeared over her palm the moment she opened her hand. Taking aim, she pulled her hand back and gave her best throw. Even though she hoped the prototype would be a success, she wasn't surprised when the fireball stuck to her hand. After she attempted to throw it a few times, the Winkies took it back to the workshop.

As the days went by, Dorothy escaped into the creative world of the Winkies and briefly forgot about the war they were preparing for. She tested more unique gadgets and weapons. Some were a complete failure, while others were perfected and produced en masse. Because everything was handmade, the Winkies made the extra effort to customize the weapons for all the guards and soldiers. Dorothy was given her own fireball thrower that fit like a second skin.

Alice, on the other hand, was not a big fan of mechanical devices. Though rotating gears had once intrigued her, she'd outgrown them the moment she'd stepped into her father's factory. To her, the sun on her face and the soldiers' shouts of enthusiasm were far more interesting. Every day, she visited the training grounds and watched people practice their fighting skills. Most of them weren't soldiers but citizens who'd arrived before her group. Born with the talent to work a sword, Alice initially found the training grounds to be a rather disappointing sight. But as the days went by, each new archer's and swordsman's improvement boosted not only her confidence but also the group's morale.

One evening, the group of men and women wielding swords challenged her to a friendly duel. Alice was a little hesitant at first but agreed to it. It wasn't really a fair fight, as her sword was shorter than theirs, but she still defeated ten people before calling it quits. At the end of the duel, her opponents praised her and cheered, and Alice could only wish for the same conclusion by Sunday.

As she returned to her tent, she ran into Brave Lion, Scarecrow, the captain, and a few other high-ranking soldiers who knew of her special request. Strangely, none of them asked what her plan to defeat the New Queen was. Instead, they all commended her for her courage before bidding her farewell. Alice wasn't sure if she should be worried or confident that everyone believed in her.

She was torn between both emotions until she bumped into Glinda, who invited her to her tent for a little teatime talk that evening. Alice expected to be asked the dreaded question, but when Glinda made no mention of it, she voiced her curiosity.

"I find it strange that no one has asked me about my plan," Alice casually said as she nibbled on a cookie.

"They have faith in you," Glinda simply replied.

"But honestly, Glinda, I don't really have a plan."

"Some things don't need a plan. I can't plan which spell to use or when to use it on the battlefield; I just have to be ready for whatever comes my way. Are you ready?"

"Yes," Alice confidently answered.

"Then treat their lack of questioning as confidence in you."

"But what if I fail?"

"Failure is in your head. The only time you truly fail is when you believe it."

It was what Alice needed to hear, and by the time she left for the night, nothing worried her anymore. Yes, there was still a war, but she had as much control over the ending as her enemy, and she was willing to place a bet on her success.

When Saturday arrived, Alice and Dorothy were called to the battle tent again. Brave Lion went through the final plan while everyone listened intently. Because Dorothy was Alice's escort, the two girls would fall back and wait for the third signal before entering Emerald City. By then, their army would have broken through the city's initial defense, and they could both easily make it to the palace. The cavalry would follow them and assist in crashing through the gates. Once they were on palace grounds, it was up to them to find the New Queen and snatch her crown.

Everything was in order. After the briefing, everyone was fired up for the next day's battle. As Alice and Dorothy returned to their tents, they couldn't remain silent.

"I'm nervous yet ready at the same time," Dorothy said.

"It's going to be hard to sleep tonight," Alice replied.

"Toto is already asleep," Dorothy said with a chuckle. She'd left him curled up in his bed when she was called to the briefing.

"Does he know he has to turn into the beast tomorrow?"

"I told him about it, so he knows. Though I'm not too sure that your potion will work. I'm just a little afraid it will be too hard to control him."

"Cheshire Cat's magic always works. You should worry more about how to manage the link."

"That's easy," Dorothy confidently said.

The two parted ways shortly after. But they'd barely shut their eyes when the day of battle arrived with the bellowing of the horn at dawn.

CHAPTER 32

Sunday mornings were always laid back in Oz, but today was unlike any other. At the sound of the horn, everyone put on their armor and left their tents, ready to face the day. They met in an open field where they formed groups according to plan. Then the older folks at the camp served them a hearty breakfast they'd made.

Alice and Dorothy joined their platoon and ate their breakfast silently. The field was filled with men and women in silver armor, and their voices rose to match the others'. Alice would have joined in to boost morale, but she was always quiet before a face-off. Dorothy also bit her tongue, but for a different reason. In her head she played out the possible scenarios she might face on the battlefield and how she would react to them. She'd done the same thing the night before, but this was like last-minute cramming for a test. Old habits died hard for the two girls.

When the plates and cups were empty, Brave Lion took his position up front. Everyone stood and waited for him to speak. It was a strange feeling for Alice and Dorothy. The last time they'd been in a world not their own, they were the ones at the front— the voice and the strength of the people. Not having the pressure of giving the last speech was rather a relief. Being a part of the crowd made them realize that anyone who fought for what they believed in was a hero. You didn't need to be the head—you just had to have a heart.

Brave Lion's speech was short and sweet. He then laid out their quick march to Emerald City. Glinda and the fairies would create portals that would bring them to their exact points. As he continued to explain the process, five large groups of fairies flew in concentric circles and blew on their palms. The fairy dust wasn't visible, but when Glinda went from one group to another, casting the same spell, silvery dust materialized to form a circle of thin, silver liquid. They made five portals, and when Brave Lion finished speaking, the fairies broke their formations and entered the portals. After a few minutes, a fairy fluttered out from each one with a thumbs-up. With the coast clear, it was time to march onto the battlefield.

The portals led to five locations around Emerald City. One portal directly faced the main gate—not right in front of the city, but near enough to see the trolls guarding the walls. By the time Alice and Dorothy stepped through the portal, the trolls had seen the crowd gathering. Their reaction was surprisingly calm as they stood their ground. A few blew monstrous horns. When the blaring of the horns reached their ears, the witches screeched a high-pitched battle cry and flew from Emerald City.

Brave Lion didn't wait for the witches to attack first. He gave a thunderous roar just as the portals shut. Green flares shot into the sky, and at the signal the first group of archers pulled back their large arrows and released them. These weren't ordinary arrows, which would wound or kill a single creature upon impact. They were specially designed to explode into a million shards of glass in midair. The arrows burst as they crested, and sharp glass rained down on the witches and trolls. It was impossible to outrun the glass as it fell in every direction.

Despite the damage from the shards, Emerald City's original residents were unharmed. The night before, they'd been informed of the impending battle by a raven in disguise. All were safely hiding in their homes, and none of them would leave till the battle was over.

After the rain of glass wounded the witches and blinded the trolls, the swordsmen charged the city. Their swords deflected the witches' spells but failed to stop the stomping trolls, as they flung their hands wildly. It was impossible for Alice and Dorothy to tell which side was winning—for every witch that fell, a soldier was crushed.

Soon, the second flare shot into the clear-blue sky. Another battle cry shook the trees and the ground as more soldiers charged the city. This time there were horses with riders wearing spiky armor. Their job was to penetrate the city as deep as they could. Hearing the stampede, the remaining witches slipped back into the city, and the few trolls left didn't put up much of a fight. Alice and Dorothy knew that behind the city walls were the New Queen's guards and her beloved muttbitts, along with the witches. It would take more than spiked armor to clear the path to the palace gates. A seed of fear took root in their hearts.

Barely a few seconds after the second signal, Dorothy said, "I think it's time for Toto to do his thing."

Alice nodded, and Dorothy picked up her dog. They walked away from the formation before she set him down and pet him.

"It's time, Toto," she said.

Toto barked in reply while Dorothy and Alice backed away, keeping their eyes on him. The soldiers in formation glanced quickly at them.

"I'm sure the cookie will work," Dorothy said. It sounded like she was trying to convince herself.

"If it doesn't?" Alice asked, knowing it was the worst question to raise at that moment.

"Then I can only hope he knows how to differentiate us from them."

Toto shivered wildly, and his fur began to grow. His transformation didn't take long—his legs cracked disturbingly while his back arched at an abnormal angle. His face changed shape, his eyes widening and his teeth lengthening. If Alice were to have faced such a beast in her dreams, she would have shot right up in bed, dripping with sweat. Nothing she saw resembled the cute, happy dog she played with. The beast that now stood in front of her was a giant, mad-looking dog with sharp claws and blood-red eyes.

When the last bone cracked into place, Toto turned to look at Dorothy and gave a low growl. Alice could feel the fear from the soldiers behind her as her throat went dry.

"Do—do something," Alice whispered in a strange voice.

"Toto!" Dorothy called. "Hush now!"

Alice wondered if that was the right way to talk to a beast like that, but she kept the thought to herself.

"Toto, it's me, Dorothy," she added as she took a bold step toward her dog.

Toto eyed her cautiously but seemed to recognize her. When she placed her hand on his jaw, he stopped growling.

"Good boy," Dorothy said with a smile that left as fast as it came. When Toto noticed Alice and the soldiers behind her, his jaws opened. He growled, showing his sharp teeth and slimy drool.

"No, Toto!" Dorothy cried.

"You have to link with him," Alice quickly said.

"How?"

"I don't know. Just do it before he kills us all!"

CHAPTER 33

Toto opened his jaws wider, threatening the friends he didn't recognize. He turned his huge head side to side, and nobody moved an inch, not even the soldiers.

"Toto, stop," Dorothy said firmly, but he didn't respond to her orders. Instead, he backed up and slowly crouched. Just as he was about to pounce, she ran in front of him with her arms wide. Toto pushed off his back legs, but to everyone's surprise he didn't make it past Dorothy. An invisible force pushed him back, and the sudden shock made him shake his head in confusion. He wasn't the only one who failed to understand what had just happened. In the midst of the confusion, Dorothy saw glimpses of herself flash in her head.

"Are you all right?" Alice asked when she noticed the befuddled look on her face.

Dorothy shook her head in reply. The flashes came so rapidly, it felt like she was looking at a flickering spotlight. When it finally stopped, her view of Toto slowly faded and merged with an image of herself. Dorothy stared blankly at the girl staring back at her before she finally realized what was going on. Her vision snapped back to Toto in front of her.

"What happened? Did it work?" Alice asked.

"I . . ." Dorothy trailed off as she noticed how still Toto was. He was no longer growling and had a calm expression on his face. She was certain the spell had worked, but before she could voice it, another set of flares shot into the sky.

"We have to go," Alice said.

Dorothy nodded and turned to Toto. She waved at him, and he bent down on his knees. Quickly they climbed onto his back. As Toto sprinted to the front line, they held on to his fur and felt a wave of exhilaration as the wind rushed over their faces.

"Are you ready?" Dorothy shouted. It was a question she addressed to all three of them.

"Ready as ever!" Alice replied, while Toto gave his assurance with what felt like a strong current of excitement that coursed through Dorothy's veins. Even though Dorothy wasn't sure she was entirely ready, her friends' strength rubbed off on her. By the time they stormed Emerald City, she truly was ready for battle.

As Toto headed toward the palace, pushing past trolls and clawing at muttbitts half his size, Dorothy saw glimpses of his actions through his eyes. Amazingly, it didn't distract her from her own mission, as each time danger appeared nearby, her senses pulled her back. They didn't need to dive into the fight because a platoon of well-trained cavalrymen followed them, but Dorothy occasionally threw a fireball while Alice swung her sword at ravens striking from above.

Once they'd successfully made it into the courtyard, they found themselves in the middle of a struggle for power. Two trolls and the New Queen's guards protected the palace gates and were fighting hard to keep them shut. It was difficult to cross the sea of people without accidentally hurting their own.

"What do we do now?" one of the soldiers asked.

"Follow my lead," Dorothy replied.

Seeing through both Toto's eyes and her own, she could take in her surroundings faster and better. When she saw an opening in the crowd where Toto could fit, Toto leapt without a word. Their link was an advantage and a challenge. Matching the point where their vision met was tricky, like a puzzle. But while it wasn't easy, Dorothy was slowly getting the hang of it.

Toto ran, the platoon following closely behind. When they were finally close enough to the gates, the platoon rode ahead and clashed with the feathered guards. Dorothy and Alice slipped off Toto and let him tackle the trolls. As he clawed at one and bit down on the other, Dorothy slashed her whip, and Alice delivered bloody cuts with her sword. The platoon meanwhile held back the feathered guards. When the trolls finally slumped to the ground, Toto crashed through the gates. Dorothy and Alice climbed onto his back, and with his paws on palace grounds, he dashed up the stairs.

"Where do you think the New Queen is?" Dorothy asked.

"Her bedchamber," Alice simply replied. She was so confident, it was as though she'd read the New Queen's mind, which scared her a little.

Dorothy knew where Queen Ozma's bedchamber was. When they stormed the great hall and barged into the ballroom, the coast was surprisingly clear. It wasn't until they reached a wide hallway leading to the New Queen's bedchamber that they found the welcoming party. Feathered guards stood almost shoulder-to-shoulder up and down the red carpet. They held their swords out, and even with them standing still, it'd be impossible to slip through without getting cut.

"I want to see the New Queen," Alice boldly said.

"She doesn't want to see you," a guard replied.

"Doesn't she want to kill me herself?" Alice asked.

Her question sent a series of whispers traveling down the hallway. They briefly stopped before they traveled again, this time from the back all the way to the front.

"The New Queen will see you if you can make it past us," the guard said.

Neither of them replied as Toto began to back away. They turned as though to leave, but when they were far enough away, Toto turned on his heels and charged at the unsuspecting guards. He managed to carry Alice and Dorothy halfway down the hall before the guards used their swords. Although they'd initially made good progress, the New Queen's elite guards kept them stuck where they were. When the number of guards finally began to thin, muttbitts joined the party, their howls bouncing off the walls.

"I don't think we can make it," Dorothy shouted to Alice.

They dismounted to give Toto a hand but couldn't handle the force of their opponents. Alice wondered if she had made a bad decision. They'd walked into a death trap so tight that escaping would be as difficult as making it through.

"We can't retreat! We can't even go back!" Alice cried as she swung her sword at a guard.

"Toto is in pain," Dorothy said.

"One last push," Alice said, almost out of breath.

Dorothy nodded and Toto pounced. He pinned five guards down but was attacked by ten more.

"We're done for," Dorothy whispered. They were three words she hoped no one heard her utter. Unfortunately, Alice caught them loud and clear, but when she turned to Dorothy, something blew the words out of her mouth before she could reply. A strong gust of wind sent them all stumbling backward. The moment after the wind passed, no one moved a muscle, including Alice and Dorothy.

CHAPTER 34

At the end of the hallway stood a figure in red. The New Queen wore a sadistically pleasant smile and a dark-red dress too simple for her on normal days, let alone in the middle of a war.

"The noise is giving me a headache," she said.

"Were you trying to sleep through it?" Alice replied.

"Oh, how rude of you. I saved your life," the New Queen said in disbelief, as though she was genuinely hurt by her words.

Alice narrowed her eyes and said, "I'm sure you believe that. Are you ready to face me now?"

"Face you? You must be mistaken. I just wanted to invite you for tea. Lunch might be a little late today."

"Very well. I'd be honored to join you," Alice said sarcastically before leaning toward Dorothy. "She won't let you wait. She'll send her guards on you," she whispered.

"We'll back up. Don't worry about us," Dorothy whispered in reply.

With a nod, Alice turned to face the New Queen and said, "My friend would like to wait over there." She pointed at the end of the hallway, and the New Queen acknowledged the unusual request with a wave.

Alice walked toward the New Queen's bedchamber, and Dorothy and Toto backed away. By the time they'd reached opposite ends of the corridor, the feathered guards had lined up between them so they could barely see each other. Craning their necks, they tried to catch glimpses of each other, knowing it could be their last time.

"Tea is getting cold!" the New Queen piped up.

"I'm sure it is," Alice said and made no further attempts to catch a peek of Dorothy and Toto. She could only hope it wasn't their final parting.

When she entered the large bedchamber, the doors closed heavily behind her. Taking a quick look around, she noticed that there weren't any guards. The New Queen must feel very confident in handling Alice by herself, but if such confidence failed her in Wonderland, it might just fail her again.

"Where's the tea?" Alice asked. She wasn't actually expecting a little tea party, but her question bought her time to take another look around.

"Tea will be served after you're dead," the New Queen replied.

Alice would have normally retorted, but she'd seen something troubling—a standing mirror with a young girl pounding the glass from within. She tried to avert her gaze the moment she saw it, but the New Queen caught her eyes darting in the opposite direction and said, "I see you've met my little friend. She was being a handful, so I made her reflect on her actions."

"And that is why you will always be hated," Alice replied.

"I should have done the same to you. If I'd taught you a lesson when you were just a child, you wouldn't have grown up to be so horrible."

"The only horror I see is you."

"Honestly, little girl. Do you really think you can defeat me?"

"As long as I'm still breathing, I'll try."

The New Queen chuckled before saying, "Since you insist, I will let you try."

Alice didn't make a move, wondering what the New Queen hoped to achieve. If it was her humiliation, she was definitely not going to let her win. Tightening her grip on her short sword, Alice slowly edged toward the bed. Just as she rested her other hand on her deck of cards, she heard a loud crash coming from outside the bedchamber. She had expected it, and when the New Queen took her eyes off Alice, Alice dove behind the bed and swiftly threw three cards at the fireplace. They bounced off at an angle and went straight for the New Queen's face. She managed to block two of the cards with a wave of her crystal hand, but one gave her a thin cut across the cheek.

"You cut me!" the New Queen cried.

Alice responded by throwing three more cards at the chandelier; they bounced and spun toward the New Queen from different angles. She waved aside the one that came straight at her face but failed to stop the other two. A couple of more thin cuts marked her arm and neck, and those minor flesh wounds infuriated her further. Alice now knew the New Queen's magic came from her hand, and she had trouble controlling her magic when she lost her patience.

"What game are you playing? This isn't chess!" the New Queen demanded. "Show yourself, pawn!"

When Alice didn't appear, the New Queen shrieked and, with another wave of her hand, flung her bed across the room. She expected to see Alice in plain view, but Alice had rolled behind a huge armchair just in time. She took five more cards and quickly threw them directly at the New Queen, who dodged a few. As the New Queen waved them away, Alice jumped from behind the armchair and swung her sword at her hand. The sword barely grazed her skin, but the New Queen shrieked anyway.

With Alice now in sight, the New Queen waved in Alice's direction, and a strong gust of wind sent Alice crashing into the dressing table. Before she could get to her feet, thin, smoky tentacles escaped from the New Queen's fingertips and curled around Alice's ankle. When they had a firm grip, they lifted Alice up and hung her upside down.

Blood rushed to Alice's head. The smoke weakened her muscles, and she lost her grip on her sword. When her vision began to blur, she forced her eyes to stay open and used the last bit of strength she could muster to reach for a card, which she threw at the smoke. Because it was laced with magic, the card sliced through the smoke like a piece of cake. Immediately, the smoke dispersed, breaking the spell. Alice landed on all fours and reached for her sword. She flung it at the New Queen, who halted it in midair. It was enough distraction for Alice to find cover. By the time the sword clanged to the ground, she was behind the flipped-over bed.

"What do you expect to fight me with, dear Alice?" the New Queen spat. "More cards?"

Alice held her breath and tried to come up with an idea. When she came up blank, she turned toward the mirror and saw the girl within gesturing at her. It wasn't hard to understand what she was motioning at. She nodded furiously when Alice touched a card. It took a few seconds to grasp what the girl was saying.

Alice pulled out a card and flung it at the mirror. It didn't bounce off like it had with the fireplace, nor did it crack the mirror upon impact, but it stuck to the mirror and made a small gap, reaching into the girl's world. The girl took a few steps back, inhaled, and screamed at the top of her lungs. The scream was so loud, the card popped off the mirror, her voice escaping into their world. It startled the New Queen, and Alice saw her chance.

She pulled her flintlock pistol from its holster, rested her hands on the bed frame, took aim, and fired.

CHAPTER 35

The bullet whizzed through the air straight toward the New Queen's hand. Both Alice's shooting lessons and the malachite potion paid off as the bullet shot through the crystal and shattered it into a million pieces. The New Queen shrieked in pain and anger as she fell to her knees. She stared at her hand in horror before attempting to gather the tiny pieces of crystal. Not wanting to lose her advantage, Alice jumped over the bed.

"You vile girl!" the New Queen shouted.

Alice saved her breath and reached for her sword, but before she could get it, the New Queen screamed, "Baby!"

Alice froze and immediately regretted she did. As the word escaped the New Queen's lips, a muttbitt crashed through the door and pounced on her. It pinned her down with its jaws wide open, but it made no move to sink its teeth into her flesh. Turning her head in the New Queen's direction, Alice could see the hallway through the frame of splintered wood. Dorothy and Toto were swiftly taking down the feathered guards and muttbitts, slowly nearing the New Queen's bedchamber.

Alice wasn't the only one who saw the guards falling to the ground. The New Queen's eyes were wide in horror as she witnessed her magic wearing off. She then snapped out of her daze and continued to search for shattered pieces of crystal on the floor. She scrambled for any piece that could be saved, including half the diamond ring. Alice didn't understand why the ring hadn't completely shattered.

While Alice tried to escape from the muttbitt's claws, the New Queen carefully picked up the fragment of the ring, muttering to herself. As the New Queen tried to regain her sanity, Alice was losing hers. She couldn't get free. Just when she was about to give up, she heard a sharp ripping sound and felt warm blood drip on her. When she realized what had happened, she gave the muttbitt a hard shove, and it fell to its side.

Alice didn't stop to thank her savior, running straight for the New Queen. As she readied to tackle her, the New Queen looked up, smiled, then transformed into a raven. The bird swiftly dodged Alice's attempt to grab it before flying out the window. Alice ran after it, but unfortunately she had no wings to chase after her enemy. When the bird dove down and disappeared from sight, she slammed her hands on the windowsill and let out a frustrated groan. The New Queen's narrow escape was unbelievable. Wondering how else it could have gone, she stood at the window, frozen in disbelief until Dorothy ran into the room.

"Your Highness!" Dorothy said when she saw Queen Ozma.

Alice turned to acknowledge the girl holding her bloodstained sword. "Thank you," she said, gesturing at the muttbitt.

"I should thank you," Queen Ozma replied and handed Alice her short sword.

Alice gave the queen a small smile and shrugged. She knew she should be celebrating the end of the New Queen's rule, but she couldn't accept the fact that her enemy had escaped.

"What happened to the New Queen?" Dorothy asked.

"She's gone," Alice replied.

"What do you mean by *gone*?"

"She escaped."

There was a short moment of silence before Dorothy broke it.

"But she is defeated, right?" she asked.

"I destroyed her magic, or at least most of it."

Alice's replies weren't very convincing, and Dorothy's and Queen Ozma's cheerful smiles faded to expressions of concern.

"Don't worry, she won't be back. Even if she tries, we'll be ready," Alice quickly added.

Surprisingly, her words seemed to appease them, and their smiles returned. The three of them left their worries with the dead muttbitt and headed to the balcony that overlooked the courtyard. When they saw the witches fleeing and the trolls being tied up, they knew the battle had been won.

• • •

That evening, after a week of horror, the citizens who were in hiding stepped out into the streets without fear. The children and old folks from the camp joined them too. Emerald City was a mess, and there were a lot of things to do, but everyone was ready to face a new day.

There was a small celebration that night at the largest tavern in Emerald City. As the bright-yellow moon rested above, Dorothy and Alice escaped the noise and climbed onto the tavern's roof. They lay on the tiles for a few minutes, silently counting the restless shooting stars in the dark sky.

After realizing they were counting the same ones over and over again, Dorothy said, "I won't be going home anytime soon. I want to help rebuild the city."

"I see," Alice replied.

"You don't have to stay—you can go home if you want," Dorothy pointed out.

"I'll stay. Besides, not a second has gone by back home."

"In that case, we'll go home together when we're ready. Oh, I almost forgot. You must give me your address," Dorothy said.

"Why? Do you want to write?"

"Why not? Maybe one day I could come visit you, or you could come visit me!" Dorothy was already excited about their next adventure.

. . .

Meanwhile, as the darkness lingered in the sky, the New Queen lurked in the tunnels below the city. When she'd escaped, she'd headed straight for the place she knew no one would find her. She couldn't risk the witches catching her or the trolls eating her, so she'd slipped into the dungeons. Once she'd felt safe, the New Queen had returned to her original form and began her aimless journey below. Even though she knew what she was looking for, she was completely lost.

The New Queen didn't know how long she wandered but knew her little diamond ring provided for her needs. She tried not to exhaust her magic, so she let her stomach growl for a few days at a time. When she finally found the place she dreamt about every night, her haggard face broke into a crooked smile.

"Finally!" the New Queen croaked.

She hurried to the center of the round chamber with the puddle of dark water. She jumped around it like a child in a toy store, then, gripping her ring tightly, she hopped right in. Scarecrow had been right to warn Dorothy—the water sucked her in like a hungry mouth. Within a split second, she disappeared. Just like that, the New Queen left Oz, never to return.

But . . . If the fairies were right, she was well on her way to another world—one you would find all too familiar.

EPILOGUE

The constant glare of a lamppost on the still, lifeless street seeped through the uneven windowpanes of a nearby house, giving just the barest light to the abandoned basement below. The basement was usually quiet, but that night something broke its peace. There was a loud thumping at the back. It went on periodically until it stopped, then the wall exploded with a loud crash. The explosion revealed a doorway that led to a hidden room. What had been shut years ago to hide a secret had now been opened from the inside by a thin figure.

The figure stumbled into the basement, knocking over boxes and shattering antiques until she found a simple candlestick. Once the candle was lit, the figure gave a sinister smile, and her eyes widened in joy. She scrambled around the dusty room in search of things she could use. She was rather lucky to find a box full of old clothes that fit her perfectly, despite its sending her into a sneezing frenzy. She changed into a white dress and a black hat, then found the flight of stairs that led up to the house.

The furniture was heavily laden with dust, and the pictures hanging on the walls were faded. Exploring the empty house, she found a mirror to check her appearance and a bathroom where she used water from a rusty tap to clean her face. When the house was no longer useful, she walked out into the empty street and began her search for revenge.

As she set out on her late-night stroll, she found a rolled-up newspaper on the sidewalk. She picked it up but couldn't read it. Words like *Munich* and *September* didn't make any sense to her. It was even more confusing when she recognized numbers, yet *September 29, 1938* looked like a secret code. The unknown was daunting, but she didn't bother trying to decipher it and continued down the cobbled street.

Hitting upon a row of shops, she found herself fascinated by one full of ticking machines. She watched a clock for a long time, not understanding how its hands pointed at one and six. Despite her cluelessness, she had to admit that this foreign land amazed her.

Knowing that she had a lot to learn before she could plot her revenge, she carried on exploring. She was tired and hungry, but the magic ring she clutched in her left hand gave her the strength to continue. She saw a poster of a man, red flags with a square black symbol on them, and a stationary, beast-like machine with wheels. The items briefly intrigued her.

After walking for an hour, she came to a tall building with a large courtyard. She spotted a bench and headed straight to it to rest her feet. As she sat quietly, watching the flickering of the nearby lamppost, the still night seemed strange to her. She hated it.

Pulling together all the things she had learned so far, she tried to piece together a plan. She had an idea who the leader of this land was, but she still hadn't figured out a scheme for revenge. Unfortunately, her current state wasn't helping. After several attempts at forming something foolproof, she gave up and got to her feet. She began to walk back to the abandoned house, though she doubted she could find it again.

As she was slowly leaving the courtyard, she heard a strange noise that got increasingly louder. Turning in its direction, she saw one of the beasts on wheels heading toward her. Curious, she stood and watched. Its lights blinded her for a second as it passed. She was amazed. She wanted it for a pet, and just as she was about to shout after it, the beast stopped. It reversed and came to a halt right in front of her. A door opened, and she heard a voice in a language she didn't understand. She answered in the only tongue she knew and surprisingly another voice asked, "Are you lost, my lady?"

She bent over to look into the car and noticed two figures seated inside. "I'm new here," she simply said.

"Where are you from?" the same man asked.

"From a land far from here," she replied.

He spoke to his companion in the foreign language, and she heard them chuckle. He then got out of the car, looking rather bemused. Cautiously, she took a few steps back.

"Why don't we take you home?" he said as he gestured for her to enter the beast.

She was now able to see the other figure much better. He looked just like the man she'd seen on the poster. He wore a suit with the square black symbol wrapped around his arm. Immediately, she knew he was important, and the plan she'd desired flashed into her mind.

The plan was simple. She would befriend this leader and give him her magical ring, then she'd convince him to find Alice and Dorothy and destroy everything they held dear. That was all she wanted, and she was determined to make it happen.

If you're curious as to whether she succeeded, just open a history book, and you'll find the answer. But consider yourself forewarned—some endings are not as pleasant as you wish them to be.

ACKNOWLEDGMENTS

God, for His prophecy.

Mom and Dad, for their heroic support and undying perseverance. My protector and defender to the very end.

Family and friends, for boosting morale on the battlefield. No weapon is greater than an army.

L. Frank Baum and Lewis Carroll, for inspiring a new adventure and drawing the map so no one could get lost.

Inkshares, for a portal into the new realm of publishing.

And you, dear reader, for your faith in the words I have written. I hope this story will not only take you on a magical journey but also gear you up to fight for what you believe in. Remember, no magic is strong enough to crush the heart of a hero.

ABOUT THE AUTHOR

Jeyna Grace never stopped playing pretend. One day, she decided to document her imagination on paper... And the rest is history.

Her first foray into the world of publishing was in 2011. Since then, she has released five titles, with two soon to be released. She also writes stories for her blog to practice her craft. She currently works for a publishing house, where she gets to create a variety of material for young readers. Their letters in response to her short stories bring her joy, but her true passion is writing novels. She dreams of becoming a full-time author one day and hopes her journey will inspire others to chase their dreams too.

Born and raised in Malaysia, she often retreats to the world inside her head, where she teaches her pet dragon to play dead.

LIST OF PATRONS

This book was made possible in part by the following grand patrons who preordered the book on Inkshares.com. Thank you.

Adrian Sia
Angelyn Looi
Cheok HP
Mr. & Mrs. Chew Kim Choon
Goo Ya Dee
Ian V. Draper
Janita Goh
Jonathan Lee
Joseph Gan Hock Han
Juriz Ibon Arcangel
Ken Wong
Mark S. W. Lai
May Ng
Michael Lee
Mohd Razik
Ngui Vun Fui
Pang Hao Lin
Peh Cheng Hee
Peter Sze
Mr. & Mrs. Roger Tan
Stephanie S. H. Teo
Tan Fui Bee
Timothy Loh
Victor Gan K. S.
Vincent Puah E. S.
Voo Hue Ling
Wong Chiew Ching
Yee Foo Giap

INKSHARES

Inkshares is a crowdfunded book publisher. We democratize publishing by having readers select the books we publish—we edit, design, print, distribute, and market any book that meets a pre-order threshold.

Interested in making a book idea come to life? Visit inkshares.com to find new book projects or to start your own.